CURSED LAIRD

CURSED MACKINNONS SERIES

BOOK 3

BY

TARA NINA

Tara Nina

Dedication

Cursed Laird is dedicated to all the honorary MacKinnon Clan members. Thank you to the readers who have shown support to the MacKinnon brothers by visiting my website and joining their cause. It is your love for them that compels me to continue writing their stories and setting them free from the dreaded Curse of the Gargoyle.

Acknowledgements

I acknowledge the love and support of my family and friends, without whom I would be nowhere in the real world. I have to admit I would've been stuck in chapter one of this book without the truly wonderful author, Cait Miller. She and I tossed story ideas back and forth on a ten-hour drive. Her knowledge of spirits and ghosts helped develop a plausible thread for this series. Thank you, Cait.

Chapter One

Deeper. Deeper. She had to go deeper. Cold cut her to the bone. Darkness surrounded her. Something lured her over the ledge. Beckoned to her soul to push beyond her limits. Caledonia knew better but couldn't stop. The words of her favorite poem urged her to descend farther.

Thy mighty Ben Lawers surrounds thee
Four rounded forts protect thy sleeping bairn
Chained within the center floats thy fourth
Safe beneath thy watchful eye of Breadalbane
Rest ye weary one fer yer day of release shall come
Lest nay be the month of one when thy favored fish of
Balloch run

The sporadic flash from her diving watch caught her attention. *Damn. Out of time.* She was *so* close. Gut instinct told her something lay at the bottom of the loch. That poem teased her with its meaning ever since she'd found it as a young child. It hinted of a great hidden treasure. She was sure of it.

When she'd finally located the one spot in the loch she hadn't plundered, the rules of diving played against her. Caledonia stared into the black abyss in the loch's deepest point. Today, time ticked against her, but tomorrow she'd be back.

Whatever you're hiding is yours for another day. Caledonia turned and slowly ascended, even though every ounce of her ached to explore that pit. To her knowledge, no one had ever ventured into it. Glancing down, she vowed whatever prize lay buried beneath its depths she'd locate and retrieve tomorrow.

Breaking the surface, Caledonia gathered her bearings then waved to her poppa, who stood fishing off the bow of their trawler, *Marcail Struana*. The moment he spotted her he lowered his pole, hauled in the anchor and maneuvered toward her. He cut the engine as soon as he reached her and helped guide her onboard.

"I was getting worried, lass," he said in his thick Scottish brogue. "You know I don't like it when you dive alone. Cutting it a bit short on your air, weren't you?"

They'd had this argument earlier when she sent the other two members of the crew, the O'Reilly brothers, on an errand. Several scuba tanks needed refills and she wanted the Trimix tanks readied in order to accomplish a dive to the bottom of the pit. At that depth she wouldn't go alone, Percy would be with her.

"Aye, but I was so close," she replied with a smile, deciding not to comment on his concern.

"Close to what, child? This ole loch's been plundered over and over. Nothing's ever been found but a few dozen bits 'n' pieces of those ancient crannogs. I think our time would be better spent searching elsewhere."

Caledonia touched his hand and met his curious gaze. Those bright, baby blues of his held a world of knowledge and she respected his wisdom, but on this she wouldn't budge. This loch called to her and she was determined to find out why.

"There's something down there, Poppa. I feel it in my gut."

"Let's pray you're right. I'd hate to think we've spent the last week trawling for nothing but fish."

As he turned to secure her scuba tank in the holder, Caledonia smiled. She knew how much he missed the fisherman's life. It saddened her to think of the decline the fishing industry suffered over the years, which caused many to leave the business. Her father included. Now, they worked as a team, trying to keep her salvage recovery company running. She asked, even though she suspected he had success from the twinkle in his eyes, "Do I take it we're having fresh fish tonight?"

"Aye," he replied with a nod toward the cooler.

Caledonia lifted the lid to the smaller of the two fish-holding tanks situated in the deck. Both were located in the stern. Four good-sized salmon lay on ice in the bin. "Looks like a good day indeed," Caledonia praised.

Poppa harrumphed good-naturedly as he readied the trawler for home. Caledonia wiggled out of her dry suit and hung it beside the scuba tank. She slipped on a light-pink cover-up over her one-piece bathing suit, gathered her notes and took a seat on the bench in the wheelhouse. With precision, she marked the coordinates of where she intended to dive tomorrow.

Flipping through the folder, she located the map of the loch and highlighted the area she'd covered in today's dive. She made note of a fishing boat she'd discovered. From the looks of its non-decayed condition, it must've been recently sunk by the last storm. Caledonia closed the file and tucked it under the cushion beneath her. She stood and walked the railing as Poppa steered for the small fishing village they called home, Lawers Glen. She'd been born there. Loch Tay was in her blood.

She scouted the shoreline, noting several homemade docks. Quite possibly, it belonged to one of those. This evening she'd post the fact she found a boat on the bulletin board at the pub. If claimed, she'd then worry about raising it.

Caledonia stared across the ripple-free water. Blue for as far as she could see, surrounded by rolling hills of green, met her approving gaze. The sun sat low on the horizon, gracing the loch with a world of phenomenal early-evening colors. The perfect setting, if she was painting a picture of serenity and beauty. Sun reflected off the glasslike surface, causing her to squint. Something lay on the bottom of Loch Tay, she sensed it. For as long as she could remember, a strange sensation tugged at her soul each time she sat along its shore. This odd calling led her to learn to dive.

Every clear day for the past week, she, Poppa and the O'Reillys prowled the loch for treasure. At night, an eerie sensation settled in her soul and kept her awake. A nagging tug deep within her, a haunting whisper on the wind tickled her fascination and lured her to search beneath the loch's surface.

Why this particular location? Why not some faraway exotic locale known for sunken ships from battles long forgotten? The questions plagued her. Caledonia sorted through her thoughts. For years she'd studied the best areas to find possible chunks of lost eras. But here… She shook her head. She'd grown up here and knew every nook and cranny of the surrounding area like the back of her hand. It was doubtful they'd find anything as Poppa claimed.

So why continue?

It had to be the history of the place, she decided. Since childhood, she'd studied Scottish history, legends and lore. There was one thing Loch Tay boasted the other lochs didn't. Crannogs. As a young girl, she remembered sitting on the dock and fantasizing about living in one of those stilted abodes. Now, she wanted to know what lay hidden within them.

A cool breeze blew across the loch. A haunting whisper followed on its lofty coattail. *Beware. 'Tis too high a price to pay for what ye seek.* Caledonia stiffened, straining to hear the words again. She shook her head, not certain if she'd heard it at all. One glance at Poppa and she knew he hadn't heard it.

Had she? Had she truly heard a whispered warning? Then it hit her as she realized the origin. Spirits walked among them, this she believed with every ounce of her being. Chin tilted, she held a defiant stance and stared across the loch. If the spirits of this land spoke a word of warning, then she knew she was right. Something lay hidden within the loch and she had to be getting close, otherwise they wouldn't have attempted to frighten her with an eerie prediction.

What price was too high? Caledonia gazed at the spot she intended to dive. Better yet, what did the spirits protect they didn't want her to find?

* * * * *

Through binoculars, he watched. What was she up to this time? He'd temporarily lost track of her after she raised that small yacht, which sank off the coast of Kinnairds Head. It amazed him she'd accomplished such a salvage feat with the beat-up trawler as her only vessel. But she did it. Probably by the strength of sheer stubbornness, he snorted. From what he'd heard, she'd received a minimal retrieval fee from the insurance company for that one. For such a paltry sum, he never would've bothered.

His company didn't retrieve common vessels for the everyday person. No. His team located and retrieved treasures sunken for centuries—long-forgotten, timeless items worth huge sums of money when sold to the right collector. He couldn't help but smirk.

Finding her in Lawers Glen, he'd thought it was some sort of joke. There wasn't anything in that loch worth finding, besides crannogs. He'd told her that every time she'd mentioned the possibility of a search and salvage expedition here. In his opinion, those weren't worth wasting time on. Nothing valuable had ever been found in one. The Crannog Society claimed them to be an ancient architectural masterpiece and turned them into a tourist spot, thus slightly stimulating the area's dying economy.

His eyebrow cocked and the corner of his lips upturned as he saw her jot notes in a folder. From past experience, he knew her methods. If she made notes, then she was on to something. But what?

The retrieval of that yacht must have restored her confidence. He dropped the binoculars to hang around his neck. Seeing the trawler turn toward shore and the dock he knew belonged to the Kavanaghs, he made his way down the hill to his car. Something in this loch held Caledonia's attention and he intended to find out what.

In all their years together, her instincts never failed them. Except once off the coast of Bermuda, he mused. Came up bust on that venture. Her claims the triangle interfered with their finding anything still annoyed him to this day. Ghost, ghouls and imaginary mystical triangles weren't real. Looting sunken treasure, now that equaled reality in his book. From the looks of what he'd seen watching Cali, his gut told him she was definitely on to something.

Now to find out what, he decided as he slid into the driver's side of his latest purchase. He sighed contentedly, sinking into the plush leather seat. Rolls-Royce truly had a way with fine leather.

* * * * *

Nothing tasted better than a Guinness after a day of diving. Caledonia tipped her glass to Poppa. "Here's to a successful day."

"Aye, lassie. That it was." He nodded in return then they each took a sip.

Regulars filled the Thistle Pub. Young and old lined the solid oak bar that ran the length of the back wall. Only a few of the ten tables around the room were occupied. Having grown up in this village, she knew everyone and they knew her. The place buzzed with chatter, laughter and a friendly game of darts. So when the door opened and the place dropped into a dead silence, she knew she wasn't going to like what she saw when she turned around.

Kip stood in the doorway. Not a blond hair out of place, or a wrinkle in his metro-chic clothes, he stared across the room directly at her. If she wasn't mistaken, his eyes were a stunning shade of blue. Guess those were the contacts of choice for the day. He looked down his nose at everyone, as if the pub was beneath his haughty standard. Which she knew in his eyes, it was. Holding his tall, lean frame in a straight-as-an-arrow stance, he maneuvered toward her, making sure not to touch anything along the way.

Able and Percy O'Reilly ended his chance of a clean, unhindered arrival by bumping into him on purpose. Caledonia couldn't help but smirk when he nearly fell on his arse from the contact. The O'Reillys made a solid wall of thick, testosterone-riddled male flesh and refused to let him pass. From where she sat, all she saw was Kip's head bobbing from side to side, trying to make eye contact with her.

"You're not welcome here, Crosby," Percy said. His Scottish brogue deepened as he stood his ground against the much smaller man. Caledonia knew if she said go, the brothers would pummel Kip to a pulp. They'd grown up together, learned to fish and dive together, and got into more trouble than she cared to remember together. They were the brothers she never had, and at the moment she contemplated letting them use Kip as a punching bag.

"That decision isn't yours to make, it's Cali's," Kip said. His voice cracked and she knew the massive brothers with their bright-red hair intimidated him. They always had when they'd worked with her and Kip at her prior salvage company.

She swallowed the smile that teased her lips. If only she were a mean person. She sighed as she stood and worked her way in between the O'Reilly boys. Being five-foot-five-inches tall and full-figured, she didn't consider herself to be a petite woman, but standing between these two made her feel small and doll-like.

"You remember the O'Reillys don't you, Kip?" she quipped.

"I remember they left the operation same time as you."

"You make it sound like I quit a job. We got divorced," Caledonia said. "They considered themselves part of the settlement."

"We didn't work for you," Percy stated, flexing his biceps. "We worked with Caledonia. Still do."

"Caledonia, you want us to throw him out?" Able asked without taking his eyes off Kip.

Seeing Kip squirm gave her momentary joy. For the first time since their divorce, she liked the look on his face. Though he tried to hide it, she knew fear raced through his veins. His gaze darted from man to man then returned to her. He wasn't a fighter. No. He was a sniveling coward of a thief. Caledonia crossed her arms over her chest and leveled a hardened gaze directly at Kip. In no way would she let him charm his way back into her life. Those boyish good looks held no magic over her anymore. Without that, he had nothing as far as she was concerned.

"What do you want, Kip?" she asked point-blank.

His Adam's apple bobbed. Sweat beaded his brow and he dabbed it with the pressed, white handkerchief he kept in the left breast pocket of his blazer. Funny, when they'd first gotten married, he wouldn't have been caught dead in one of those. Though she hated to admit it, he smelled nice. The cologne she recognized as her favorite and knew it was expensive. Just like everything else he tended to own over the last few years of their marriage. *Nothing was too good for Kip Crosby.* The memory of his words slid through her brain and tightened her spine.

He hadn't always been so self-centered and arrogant. Caledonia remembered for a split second the younger version of Kip, the one she fell in love with who enjoyed the adventure of the hunt. Then the reason that busted their marriage reared its ugly head as she perused the expensive clothing he wore. The moment they struck a rich find, his motive switched to money. It became about the money and nothing else with him, and that just wasn't her thing. It killed whatever love she'd felt for him.

"I..." He licked his lips. She could tell he was nervous. His tongue slurred his words and his cockney accent slipped past his usual prim 'n' proper British demure. "I heard you scored a retrieval credit for your new salvage company off Kinnaird's Head."

"It didn't make the papers," she said. "How'd you find out?"

"Come on, Cali. You know how small the salvage community is. Word spreads quickly." She noted his tone changed as he flashed a perfect white smile then poured on the charm. "Thought I'd drop by and congratulate you."

"You could've called," she retorted.

"You wouldn't have answered."

"A card would've sufficed."

"You would've thrown it away."

"More than likely, torn it up and burned it," Percy interjected, cracking his knuckles as he pressed one of his meaty fists into the palm of his other hand.

Kip instantly stepped back. His eyes widened and he looked as if he'd bolt for the door at any second. Though she loved the subtle torment of her ex, she decided to be the bigger person and save him from annihilation—for now.

"You've said your congratulations. Is there anything else?"

"I could use a drink. What do you say to you and I having a drink together for old time's sake?"

Caledonia studied his face. With those striking blue contacts in, she couldn't read him. Was he telling the truth or did he want something? Hell, he got practically everything in the divorce—with the exception of the O'Reillys. What else could he want? Though she knew better, curiosity got the upper hand. She sidestepped Able and drew out a chair at the closest empty table.

"Have a seat." She waved her hand at the table as she sat. When Percy and Able both moved to sit as well, she shook her head then tossed her thick, jet-black braid over her shoulder to lay down the center of her back. "I think I've got it from here, boys. You'll hear me scream if I don't."

The pair nodded then strode to the bar, leaned against it but didn't take their sea-green eyes off Kip. She noted Poppa had turned and leaned with his back to the bar, staring straight at them. Kip was not his favorite person and she couldn't blame him. He wasn't hers either.

"What's the real reason you're here, Kip?" When he reached for her hand on the table, she dropped it to her lap. There was no reason for contact.

"You're the reason I'm here, Cali." His shortened version of her name used to give her chills and make her smile. Now, it grated on her like a Siamese cat's meow. "I miss you."

"You miss *me* or my talent?" Caledonia nearly snorted on her reply. "What's the matter, Kip? All the *hot* leads dried up? That tight little first mate of yours can't read well enough to research the history books, and help you locate possible sunken treasures on a map?"

Kip straightened in his chair. The muscle in his jaw ticked and she knew she'd hit a sore spot.

"I can see you're still angry with me over my employment of Lillianna," Kip said. Though his tone seemed calmer as he spoke, she noted he continually checked Able's and Percy's location over her shoulder.

"Actually, I couldn't care less who you employ."

His expression brightened and she knew she was right. He came for a specific reason and not a social visit. "Then would you consider employment with Marine Treasures Salvage?"

Uninhibited laughter burst from her. She couldn't believe he'd said that. He offered her employment with the company she helped build from the ground up. His face reddened and she swore she saw steam rise from his head. Wiping the tears from her eyes with a napkin, she cleared her throat. "You're kidding, right?"

Kip's chin tilted and he gave a slight nod when he replied in a cold tone, "I never joke about a job offer."

"Considering what we've been through…" She let her voice trail as she leaned forward and got as close to his face as she could stand. It turned her stomach to see him prepare as if she meant to kiss him. Caledonia swallowed the disgust that threatened to rise, and on a heated breath clearly voiced her decision. "The answer is no."

* * * * *

Hours into the night, Caledonia researched her notes, scoured the Internet and studied the history of Loch Tay. Dead tired, she flopped onto her pillow, leaving everything scattered on her bed. Nothing magically appeared. No clues as to what lay hidden beneath the surface. Instinct demanded she dive again tomorrow. Excitement toyed with her brain, causing her to remain awake, though she desperately needed to sleep.

Something tickled her thoughts and kept her brainwaves frantically searching for an answer. The words of her favorite poem took center stage.

Thy mighty Ben Lawers surrounds thee

Four rounded forts protect thy sleeping bairn

Chained within the center floats thy fourth

Safe beneath thy watchful eye of Breadalbane

Rest ye weary one fer yer day of release shall come

Lest nay be the month of one when thy favored fish of Balloch run

Caledonia sat upright, nearly sending her laptop crashing to the floor. Why hadn't she seen this before? It suddenly made sense. Shuffling through her thoughts, she remembered the day she'd found it. The spirits gave her a stiff warning that day as well. She remembered running from what she'd thought was an angry banshee when she was a child. Until now, she hadn't thought much about it.

While playing on the outskirts of the main grounds of Castle Taymouth, she and the O'Reilly brothers stumbled on a forgotten root cellar. The memory of Able falling through the rotted doorway into a pitch-black hole made her snort. That's when they learned he was scared of the dark. She and Percy quickly lit a makeshift torch of dried grass and sticks then scrambled inside with Able. They used their torch to light several partially melted candles they found secured in sconces on the wall.

The simple memory of the root cellar brought a cool sensation to her skin and the smell of dirt, mud and stale air teased her olfactory senses. Funny how strong a memory could be. She smiled, thinking through that day's adventure.

They spent hours exploring the root cellar. The boys' sampled ale they found still corked in bottles and lined on the shelves. One didn't contain liquid. She discovered a parchment rolled and hidden in an old ale bottle. The cork disintegrated when she tugged it free. The screech of a banshee sent her and the boys running from the cellar. She dropped the bottle, but held on to the parchment as she ran. The boys took off through the woods but she didn't stop until she was safely in her room.

She remembered being out of breath as she dropped upon her bed. The memory of the screech echoed in her head, causing her to shiver. *Get out! Take nothing with ye least ye be cursed as well.* When she'd finally shaken off the banshee's attack, she read the parchment for the first time. Written upon it were words she didn't understand but would never forget.

She realized these words haunted her and kept drawing her back to Loch Tay. No matter how many great treasures she and Kip had found over the years, something always hinted she'd missed one.

Was it hidden in this poem?

Caledonia walked across the room to her dresser. One glance at her reflection and she knew she was severely in need of rest. A pair of cerulean eyes stared back at her. Underneath lay a set of dark circles. She rubbed her tired eyes.

Sleep is overrated. She took a cleansing breath.

She opened the top drawer and lifted the parchment from its hiding place. It was in great shape, considering its age. Even as a child she'd known its worth and had gently pressed it in wax paper, as if it were a delicate flower she wished to keep forever. It took patience and a Gaelic dictionary to help her read the words and etch them in her memory.

A chill skittered down her spine and along her arms just as it had the first time she'd translated the ancient Gaelic script. She rubbed her arms against the sudden coolness that graced her skin. Were the spirits in the room with her? Since the day she found the parchment, she sensed a soul from the past kept an eye on her. But why? What did it want with her? Caledonia's eyes widened. Or did it guard this poem for some reason?

That banshee didn't scream at them until she uncorked the bottle containing the parchment. Closing her eyes, she tried to envision the shape she'd seen hovering in the root cellar. Was it an angry banshee, or simply a woman's ghost protecting something that belonged to her? Caledonia shrugged as she opened her eyes. The memory was so faded she couldn't determine much about the image, but the words of warning, she'd never forgotten.

She took the poem and crawled into bed among the array of research materials. Quickly, she flipped through the book on Scottish history. Something she thought she'd seen piqued her interest. She skimmed the pages until she found exactly what she needed. Balloch Castle once stood almost exactly where Taymouth Castle now stood. According to the dates she found, it was torn down around 1805.

Funny, she'd lived here her whole life and never paid much attention to its history. For years, she'd worked to dissect tidbits of history pertaining to sunken ships around the world in order to locate them. She'd never thought to read about her native area. Was there a sunken treasure in Loch Tay? She leaned against the headboard and closed her eyes. Line by line she deciphered the poem inside her head.

Thy mighty Ben Lawers surrounds thee

She knew Ben Lawers was the mountain range surrounding Loch Tay. Its beauty added to the perfect backdrop for a loch. The phenomenal network of hiking and winding bike paths through its rolling hills helped attract tourists. Not to mention the crannogs. The second and third sentences, she easily dissected.

Four rounded forts protect thy sleeping bairn
Chained within the center floats thy fourth

The remnants of every crannog found so far were round. She sat upright and gathered her notepad. What if these two lines pertained to crannogs in the loch? She drew a diagram of her thoughts, placing four round crannogs in a circle with a fifth in the middle. Could it possibly be some sort of fortification guarding something? But what? Caledonia grabbed her map of the loch and compared the locations of where known crannogs existed with the spot she intended to dive in the morning. Her heartbeat increased. It sat dead center of where four crannogs had been located.

She lifted the parchment and reread the second line to make sure she wasn't remembering it incorrectly. A sleeping bairn? What did a sleeping child have to do with this? Caledonia sat back, perplexed for a moment. That part confused her so she shook it off and continued.

Safe beneath thy watchful eye of Breadalbane

According to the history book, the Campbells of Breadalbane owned the vast majority of land holdings in the area, including Balloch Castle. Could it be that this particular clan watched over something—something they hid within a crannog in the center of the loch? Caledonia's brain clicked, trying to piece the puzzle together.

Rest ye weary one fer yer day of release shall come

Rest weary one for your day of release shall come? Her brow bunched. Had they placed a child inside a crannog for some particular reason? Was this poem not about a treasure, but the death of a child and the spot they buried him? Her heart sank. Was she about to plunder a child's grave? She stared at the last line of the poem and confusion swirled again.

Lest nay be the month of one when thy favored fish of Balloch run

The favored fish of Balloch was the salmon, which ran every January. Fishermen from all over still visited Loch Tay in January for the best salmon fishing around.

"Okay," she whispered aloud as she gathered her thoughts. Maybe this poem didn't mean anything. Maybe a distraught mother, who lost her son, wrote it and they placed him in a crannog as his tomb. Great. She sighed. She'd been hooked on a death poem thinking it meant something phenomenal lay hidden in the bottom of the loch.

Caledonia got out of bed and paced. She walked to the window and opened it, hoping the fresh air would clear her head. From her room, she had the best view of the loch. Moonlight glittered across its surface, giving it a romantic appeal, which made her smile.

Breathing deep, she took in the soothing coolness of the night and sighed her exhale. Silence filled the air. Nothing moved except the breeze. All was peaceful for as far as she could see, so she knew the quiet fishing village rested for the night.

A yawn overtook her and she decided she needed sleep. When she reached to close the window, the breeze gave her one last gift, but not a peaceful one. A whisper in the form of a sweet, feminine voice rode on its wings and taunted her tired brainwaves.

Find him, save him. 'Tis time.

Caledonia froze, knowing the spirits reached out to her. Find who? Where? As reality hit, she slowly turned and stared at the parchment on her bed. Did they want her to find this lost bairn? If so, why, and who was he?

She stood at the side of her bed and lifted the parchment. In the lower, left-hand corner, she noted a tiny marking she hadn't noticed until now. Squinting, she made out a year—1740. Oh God, this was over two hundred years old. She gathered her notes and the rest of the research papers and moved them to her desk. She slid into bed and snuggled under her covers.

Thoughts hummed inside her head, not letting her rest. Nowhere in her research had she found any information on a favored Campbell son's death. And after two hundred years, what was the possibility she'd find anything left of this lost child anyway? Entombed in a crannog, which sank from years of decay. What a way to be buried. Was he alive when they placed him in this crannog?

It did say chained within the center floats the fourth. Did being chained within the center mean this bairn was a criminal of sorts? Did they chain him inside a rotted old crannog to drown when the floor caved in? And what in the world did fourth have to do with it? Caledonia rubbed her eyes and prayed her thoughts ceased this line of subject matter. Death disturbed her. She didn't like it when people died, and if she was right, it seemed someone who died was chained in the center of a crannog.

A weak laugh escaped as she tried desperately to rein in her imagination. There had to be another answer. And tomorrow… She exhaled heavily. Tomorrow she'd find the truth when she dove.

Chapter Two

With Trimix tanks ready, Caledonia slipped on her dry suit. She'd calculated the depth and knew they needed the special mixture these tanks provided and their rebreathers to reach bottom. Carefully, she cleaned the most important part of their antiquated sonar equipment, the towfish. She planned to drop it over the side and guide it directly into the deepest spot of the loch. Usually, they simply towed it behind the boat, but not today. She needed it set in a specific location in case they ran out of time before finding anything.

An early-morning rainstorm had passed through and darkened the usually blue waters with a murky hue. She and Able lowered the towfish over the side. Slow and steady, they released the cable until it struck bottom.

"You should probably wait a day for the water to settle," Poppa said as she checked her gear, calculated her air and set the timer on her watch.

"We won't be long, Poppa. I promise." She nodded at Percy. "You ready?"

"Aye," Percy replied.

Poppa helped her with her scuba tank. "I'll be waiting. No need to fish today. Nothing biting with the water stirred into a soupy mess."

"You never know. It might be the perfect day to catch Devil's Disciple." She winked at him right before she situated her mask and adjusted her regulator.

Poppa's harrumph followed her over the side. "Me and every other fisherman's been chasing that salmon for years. He's a smart one he is. Besides, no one fishes on a day like today. Water's too murky."

Floating in the water, she asked right before she situated the regulator in her mouth, "Think maybe he hasn't been caught because no one's tried on a murky madness day?"

He handed her the underwater camera, which she clipped to her equipment belt. She lived for her time beneath the water. Peace bloomed below the surface and opened a world of possibilities. She took the lead. In slow, solid strokes, she cut through the murk following the anchor chain to the floor. Every few feet, she attached a glow stick to light their return path. The closer she got to the bottom, the less murky it appeared.

An euphoric sensation gloved her. The beat of her heart increased with anticipation of what she might find. The water underworld loved her and she it. Slow and steady, she descended, equalizing with each new depth. At thirty meters, she rested, allowing her system to adjust. Fish swam past. Percy pointed to a trophy-sized salmon that skirted within a foot of them, causing her to smile inwardly and think of Poppa's reaction if he'd reeled in that one.

Underwater, nothing bothered her. Peace filled her soul and guided her toward the bottom. Meter by meter, she swam, taking in everything the scenery provided. A multitude of fish varieties entertained while she searched for the ledge. Fifty meters put them within arm's length of the floor. If they didn't each have a light, decent visibility wouldn't exist. Even with the flashlights, eyesight fell to within a few feet. Temperatures dropped. Thank goodness they wore dry suits or hypothermia would set in and cut their exploration time in half.

She planted a glow stick at the base of the anchor chain. Percy attached a line to the towfish. Side by side, they pushed off in the direction she needed to head. Slow, methodical strokes had her hovering at the ledge within minutes. Caledonia positioned her light and scanned the darkness. Nothing significant appeared. Then again, she doubted it would. Not at this depth. According to her calculations, the bottom of this pit in the floor equaled Loch Tay's deepest point, which was close to five hundred feet—her maximum diving depth.

A sense of pride welled within her at knowing she was one of an elite circle of women to have accomplished such a feat. It had taken both she and Percy several years of training to qualify as technical divers, which allowed them to reach greater depths than recreational divers.

Excitement coursed through her as she eased over the ledge. With the help of the light and the telephoto lens, maybe she'd get some sort of pictures. With the towfish attached to the utility line of his belt, it followed Percy into the pit.

Together, they did a slow decline. Depth by depth she rested to adjust and equalize to the pressure. She knew her limits and didn't plan to push it. Slowly and surely, they lowered into the darkness, until the cable connecting the towfish to the boat ran taut. They were out of line, which meant they'd reached approximately four hundred feet. A glance at her watch confirmed the depth.

She attached two glow sticks to the base of the towfish. Then clipped the end of the retractable utility line from her belt to the towfish cable as an added measure of security for finding their way back if they got lost. Camera in hand, she maneuvered lower and directed the light straight down. Caledonia snapped pictures in multiple directions. She strained to see through the camera, but nothing came into clear focus. An oddly shaped object resting in the shadows of the loch teased her optic perception. She blinked and it disappeared.

Had she truly seen it? She motioned to Percy, who then dove lower. She followed.

Anticipation sizzled in her gut. Her chest tightened. Caledonia moved in the direction she thought she saw something. Lower and lower she sank. Icy coldness cut her to the bone even through her dry suit. Her watch flashed the depth as four hundred fifty feet. Pressure pounded in her ears as her heartbeat increased. It was close. She felt it. Something sat on the outer edge of her visual perception.

Go deeper. Save him. The words echoed inside her head. Caledonia hurriedly glanced from side to side in search of the sound she swore she heard. No one other than Percy swam near. At this depth, she knew they were alone. Few divers went beyond recreational limits unless specifically trained for extreme conditions. Caledonia remained buoyant and still, forcing her thoughts and breathing to calm. Rapid breaths wasted air, which was foolish.

She closed her eyes and let the peace of the surroundings wash over her. Once she calmed her system, she opened her eyes and read the concern in Percy's eyes as he hovered directly in front of her. When she gave the signal she was fine, they continued.

Within a short distance, she saw an obscure semicircle. As she got closer, she noted the remnants normally associated with a crannog were not discernable. There were no wooden pilings or rocks piled as the crannog's base. Instead it appeared as if this abode were built differently, like a round sort of boat that floated into this area. From its condition and the amount of underwater life and vegetation surrounding it, this sank many years ago.

Carefully she studied what was left of the wall. On one section of a wooden plank she found loops from a chain. She glanced at her watch to gain her bearings, then noted its depth and direction. If memory served her, this side faced one of the crannogs known to have existed near the southern shore. Was this proof from the poem? If she followed a straight line from here to the shore, would she find more of this chain? Would it have been attached to that crannog? Was her theory correct?

Chained within the center floats thy fourth

The words teased her senses. Blood whooshed through her ears and again she had to calm herself and focus on keeping her breathing slow. *Don't waste air. Remain calm.* If she got too excited, Percy would make her surface and she wasn't ready. Caledonia crossed the remains of the wall and flashed the light into the center.

My God, what was that?

Was it a man? Scanning the light over it, she couldn't believe what she thought she saw. She swam closer. It didn't move. And for good reason. She realized it was a statue. Caledonia circled the solid slab. In painstakingly slow movements, she gently removed vegetation and silt from the face of the statue. While Percy held their lights focused on it, she took pictures from every angle. No one was going to believe this find without picture proof.

A closer inspection of the statue's face made her heart skip a beat. He was handsome in every aspect, strong chin and jawline, but his eyes held her mesmerized. If they were real, she swore they'd show a world of emotion. The look upon his face was a mixture of sadness, surprise and anger. Lowering her gaze, she noted his hand upon the hilt of a partially drawn sword. His stance was that of a man about to lunge into battle.

Percy tapped her shoulder and motioned to his wrist then gave her the signal it was time to ascend. A check of her gauge reiterated it. An ache grew inside her. She didn't want to leave. Yet, she knew she had no choice. Years of dive training forced her to follow the rules—rise slow and steady from extreme depths, exhale evenly, stop every few meters to equalize.

Caledonia felt compelled to touch his face. She cupped his cheek and wished he were real. Shocked at herself, Caledonia pushed away from her find. Great. She should've known the perfect man existed only in statue form. Turning, she scanned the area with the light and noted the wall appeared to have been rounded in shape, enclosing the statue like a protective barrier. It was smaller in size than any of the other crannogs. Maybe it was specifically built to house this statue in some sort of houseboat-type structure. But why?

Had they actually floated a crannog to the center of the loch? If she proved this theory, it would add another vital page of information in the history of crannogs and Loch Tay. Caledonia smiled inwardly. Was this the break her company desperately needed?

The discovery of one simple artifact would lift their small-time salvage operation from the dredges of the unknown and catapult them onto the front page of *Archeology Today*. Her accomplishments had been on the front page of that magazine more than once. Each article belittled her involvement in the discoveries of several substantial shipwrecks, and gave the glory to her ex-husband, Kip. The mere image of his boyish good looks flashed behind her eyes, causing her teeth to grind against the regulator.

Thief. The man was nothing more than a pompous, self-absorbed thief. Claimed every discovery as his. Hell! He didn't even like to dive past recreational limits. Heat boiled in her gut as she closed her eyes and forced the rising anger to subside. *Don't waste air. Remain calm.* Besides, it wouldn't do to dwell in the past. Nothing good ever came of it.

Caledonia shook her head as she followed Percy and the towfish cable out of the dark crevice, leaving the statue behind. As she reached the ledge, she glanced back in the direction of the perfect man. Unwarranted sadness filled her soul because she had to leave. Every ounce of her wanted to stay and explore the ruined abode and study her latest find.

At the top of the pit, she released the towfish cable they'd used as a guideline. The pale-green light of the glow sticks led them to the anchor chain. A muffled clank broke the silence of the water. Chin tilted, she spotted the murky shadow of the large cowbell Poppa used to notify her of problems on the surface. One clank equaled visitors. Two notified her of equipment issues that required her to return to the boat.

Since another clank didn't immediately follow, Caledonia focused on the surface. They ascended as fast as feasibly possible. Percy pointed to the hazy shape of a boat's bottom floating alongside the *Marcail Struana*. Not large. An outboard motor positioned at the rear hinted of a fishing boat.

Caledonia took no chances. She attached the camera to the anchor chain out of sight of the surface. Not sure who visited, good or bad, she decided to keep the evidence of their exploits secret. Breaching the water as if nothing were amiss, Caledonia signaled to Poppa they'd arisen. He scurried to her assistance, taking the scuba tanks and fins. She grabbed the ladder and made her way onboard, followed by Percy.

The moment she gained her balance, the hairs on the back of her neck stood on end. She crossed the deck to where Able stood as if he guarded against invasion. She looked over the side. Kip sat in a fishing boat, smiling at her.

"What do you want?" she snapped.

"You." His one word answer and the smug, I'm-too-sexy-for-myself look on his face turned her stomach. Today's eye color—aqua.

"I told you last night, I'm not interested in your job offer."

"Listen, Cali," he said. "Be reasonable. I know you're not doing well in the business right now. Let me help you."

She tugged the dry suit off her shoulders and let it hang around her waist. Underneath she wore a one-piece, plain green bathing suit. She crossed her arms over her chest and stared directly at him. "How we are doing is none of your concern. Now shove off."

"You want me to hop over the rail and knock some sense into him?" Able asked. Before she could answer, Kip made a fool of himself.

He stood too quickly, making the smaller boat wobble. His comedic movements to remain in the boat without turning it over almost made her laugh. In his presence, she refused to smile. That didn't stop Able and Percy from making fun of him.

"For a salvage king, as you claim yourself to be, you've got the sea legs of an ostrich," Percy shouted before he laughed loudly along with Able.

Once he gained his balance, she read the anger mixed with embarrassment in his expression. He prided himself on being a top salvage entrepreneur. She knew it wasn't in him to do the hard work. All he wanted was the glory and a chance to sell whatever was found to the highest bidder. It killed her inside to know what he'd done with several historical artifacts she wanted to donate to a museum. Caledonia tilted her chin and forced her anger to subside. She couldn't change the past, but she'd be damned if she'd let him interfere with her future.

"I know you're up to something, Cali. Let me help." He widened his eyes, trying to look like a large-eyed puppy but failing. In their younger days, that would've worked, but not now. Age lines were more pronounced when he did this and she wondered if he knew just how pitiful he looked. "What did you find? I can see it in your eyes. You're on to something."

"What I'm up to is none of your business." She cut a glance across her shoulder. Poppa held a loaded spear gun in hand. When he leveled it over the side at Kip, she watched the color drain from Kip's cheeks. Gone was the flirtatious Kip, now she read fear in his eyes. "As you can see, Poppa's not forgiven you for the way our marriage ended. If I were you—"

She didn't get to finish. Poppa shot the spear through the bottom of the fishing boat directly between Kip's feet. Water flowed in rapidly.

"You crazy old fool," Kip screamed as he scrambled to start the outboard motor. "You could've killed me."

"Believe me, Kip, he doesn't miss what he aims for," Caledonia stated, leveling a cold stare his way.

"That was a warning," Poppa claimed as he reloaded the spear gun. "The next shot's aimed for your *little* head."

Caledonia never saw Kip move so fast. One massive pull of the cord fired the motor to life. He didn't even sit before he cut the boat away from the *Marcail Struana* and headed straight for the closest shore. Laughter burst from them as they stood watching him try to control the boat as well as bail water to remain afloat.

Several moments passed before any of them gained control. Caledonia hugged her poppa. "I love you."

"Aye, lass. I love you too." He returned her hug then turned to put the spear gun away.

"Nice shot, Mr. Kavanagh," Able claimed as he patted Poppa on the back.

"Doubt he'll take the hint," Percy said as he shrugged out of his dry suit. "That one's a snake."

"Aye, there're more spears where that one came from," Poppa bragged. "Next one's aimed for his balls."

Caledonia shook her head as she walked to the anchor chain and reached beneath the water level to retrieve the camera. There were pictures on there she couldn't wait to show Poppa and Able, since they weren't on the bottom and didn't get to see the statue.

Able removed a towel from the sonar screen. When she raised an eyebrow he shrugged. "Didn't think he needed to see what we saw."

"Good thinking," she praised. "Have you been getting a decent signal? It's near bottom." She crossed her fingers and said a prayer the older-model refurbished sonar equipment didn't fail right now.

Able nodded as he pointed to different shapes on the screen. "It looks like you found something rather large, here in the center. From what I can tell, you may have found another crannog."

"You're right. I think we've made a major discovery."

She removed the memory card from the camera and slid it into her laptop. While she waited for it to load, she studied the sonar images. The image was clear. A large, human-shaped object appeared. Granted, it was simply a dark blotch on the screen but she knew. She knew it was a phenomenal find. Who posed for this statue? Was he famous? And most of all—what was his position in Scottish history?

Caledonia documented the find on the map and in her notes. The images were stored in the sonar's computer along with its exact location. As soon as Poppa set the automated reel for the towfish cable at a slow steady pace for rolling it in, she made him sit beside her. Together they studied the pictures from the camera.

"Looks to me like you found another crannog. That's not much to be excited about," Poppa stated.

"It's not the crannog, it's what's inside," she claimed, pointing to the statue that appeared in the next picture.

"What's that?" Poppa asked.

"It's what I hope will put us on the map in the salvage business, Poppa."

* * * * *

It had been a long night of preparations and little sleep. Every time she closed her eyes, the handsome face of the statue filled her thoughts. Strange dreams kept waking her. A voice she deemed as a spirit kept urging her to save him. Several times during the early-morning hours, she thought she saw the image of a woman in her room. But when she sat up, no one was there. She shrugged it off as being her overactive imagination compounded with the excitement of her find.

Spirits spoke to her, this she believed. But why would they surround this particular bit of stone? And why was it so important she *save him* as the voice requested on each whispered plea? She swore it was the same voice that warned of a curse if she continued. Why'd it change its tune? That was a mystery she was determined to figure out.

Before the sun broke the horizon, Caledonia and her crew dropped anchor above their latest treasure. Poppa and the O'Reillys worked tirelessly lowering the equipment necessary to bring the statue to the surface. If she'd calculated right, the half-ton jib crane on the *Marcail Struana,* along with the airbags she intended to attach to the statue should be sufficient to haul her prize aboard. By mid-morning, she and Percy were suited up and over the side.

Knowing its exact location shortened the time it took to reach it. With precision, they attached the deflated airbags. Once full, the airbags would rise to the surface and if placed properly, the statue would follow along with them. Around the statue's middle, she and Percy wrapped a harness then attached it to the cable from the jib crane. She checked and double-checked the placements. Satisfied everything was ready, she released the red rubber ball from her belt. It floated to the surface and served as a signal for Poppa and Able to start the air compressors.

Caledonia remained with the statue, checking the bags and the tension on the jib crane cable. Percy kept an eye on the compressor lines to the airbags. Both knew this would take hours for the bags to fill. The lines were set. Air reached the bags and the filling process started. There was nothing left for them to do but ascend and watch the onboard gauges for signs of trouble and wait.

She faced the statue. Those silent eyes spoke to her soul. Something in them made her ache to remain at his side and guide him to the surface. She knew she couldn't, not with the limited equipment she owned. If she had the two-man submersible Kip won in the divorce, escorting this treasure wouldn't be a problem.

The use of a rebreather helped give her a greater depth range, but even when used with tanks containing the trimixure—a blend of oxygen, helium and nitrogen-time was limited. Most tanks allowed approximately two to two-and-a-half hours of underwater exploration before surfacing was mandatory. It would take longer than that for the statue to breach the surface thus making it impossible for her to accompany it. With one last look, she turned and reluctantly followed Percy to the surface.

Hours passed before the tension on the jib crane cable went lax. Her heart skipped a beat as she stared over the rail. That meant either the cable detached—which she doubted—or the airbags had filled enough to cause the statue to lift. Able manned the jib crane. She exhaled when the cable tightened. It was a sign the statue remained attached. A check of the gauges showed the bags were near maximum capacity.

Slow and steady, Able maintained the jib crane. The cable returned to the reel at inch-by-inch intervals. When she saw the hazy outline of the airbags, she knew the statue had to be close behind. The moment the airbags broke surface, she and Percy were over the side. Silently she prayed the jib crane didn't fail.

Able kept the line taut. Their timing needed to be precise. If they released the airbags from the statue too soon, it might sink if the cable didn't hold. Once she and Percy were in place, she signaled Able. The most beautiful sight she'd ever seen revealed itself within several feet of her. Effortlessly the jib crane lifted the statue from the water. As it breached the surface, Poppa hooked the harness with a gaff and helped steady it so the airbag lines could be detached.

Quickly, Caledonia and Percy removed the airbags, opened the air valves and hooked the lines together, then attached them to the drag cable that would reel them back onboard once the air had been released. By the time they finished, Poppa and Able accomplished landing the statue on deck safely.

Caledonia and Percy climbed onto the trawler. She couldn't believe how easily they succeeded in this retrieval. Not a hitch. Carefully, Poppa removed the harness and jib crane cable. Each inspected their treasure.

"He needs a good cleaning," Poppa stated.

"Aye," Percy said, "not like we haven't done that before."

"I'm thinking this statue's no ordinary structure," Able stated.

"Why's that?" Caledonia asked absently as she studied the handsome piece.

"Unless the gauges of the jib are off," Able said with a shrug, "then this isn't as heavy as the calculations suggested."

Her brow bunched. "Think it's hollow?"

Poppa pressed his ear against it and rapped his knuckles on the stone. "Nay, it doesn't sound it."

"What'd it weigh once it broke surface?" she questioned. It didn't make sense. From the measurements she'd taken and the dimensions given by the sonar, she calculated it should've weighed in at approximately five to six hundred pounds.

"Two-fifty."

"No way," she gasped. What was it made of?

Caledonia ran her hand along the frozen length of arm. *Strong biceps.* She paused at its face, cupping its cheek in a tender caress. Gently she brushed a bit of bottom crude from its lips. *So kissable.* She stepped back. What was wrong with her? Fantasizing over a statue. But it didn't stop her from lowering her gaze to his kilt.

She shook her head and turned away. "We need to get him cleaned up. Maybe there's a mark somewhere on him as to who sculpted him and when."

Able and Percy hauled the airbag gear aboard as Poppa weighed anchor.

The sun sat low on the horizon. Caledonia flopped onto the bench as the *Marcail Struana* headed for home. Staring at the statue, something bothered her. She couldn't put her finger on it, but she knew there was something different about this find. It didn't fall into the normal category for weight. So what was it made of? What type of stone appeared heavy but weighed less? Where'd it come from?

An image appeared beside the statue. Caledonia blinked but the image remained. She looked at the men and knew they didn't see it. Should she point it out? Before she could speak, the image took the shape of a petite woman dressed in ancient Scottish garb. A chill coated Caledonia's exposed skin as the spirit floated closer.

"Ye have found him. Thy lost bairn has returned." The words whispered from its lips and Caledonia's eyes widened. It actually spoke directly to her right before it disappeared. Her chest tightened with the realization no one else heard it.

Why only her? Why not the others?

She lay on her side on the bench and stared at the statue. It had to be the excitement of the find setting her imagination off the deep end. That and the fact she was exhausted. She exhaled heavily, trying to clear her head. But the thoughts wouldn't slow. She'd accomplished a major dive and retrieval today. That was something to be proud of so why was she seeing things? Was it some sort of ill effect from the deep depth? Thinking through the dive, she knew she'd followed all safety precautions. Percy wouldn't let her rise too fast. She had to give him that. He was overcautious to a fault.

Spirits spoke to her, this she believed, but never like this and never at such a close distance. It had always been simple, disembodied voices, which whispered to her psyche. Caledonia closed her eyes and tried to rest.

There was much work to be done when they reached dock. Now was not the time to let the spirits make her batty.

* * * * *

Castle MacKinnon, Lochsbury, Grampian Mountains

For days, Akira felt a disturbance in the ethereal essence of the dead. A strange sensation filled the air around her. Something gnawed at her, keeping her on edge. Did this mean her family was close to finding another *brathair*? Two of her brothers were free. They'd left the castle several days prior to journey deep into the Grampian Mountains in search of the ruins of a long-forgotten church.

Her *brathair* Ian's fiancée, Izzy, stumbled upon a picture on the Internet in some couples' photos of their hiking trip through the Grampian Mountains. It showed a statue in the overgrown garden of this church. Though it wasn't a great picture, it did resemble what might possibly be a cursed brother. After contacting the owners of the picture, they calculated their route. Unfortunately, most of it would be by foot.

The woman who befriended Akira after she purchased MacKinnon Castle, May, took her English Springer, Belvedere, and went to London for an art show. According to an article she read, a private collector was displaying an entire collection of Irish and Scottish antiquities. In the listing of the items for the show was a set of statues labeled as the *sleeping twins*. Akira knew May was hopeful she'd found the youngest of the MacKinnon *brathairs*, the twins Donnell and Dour.

Akira spun around at the sound of a creak in the castle then laughed at her silliness. Being a ghost, nothing could harm her any more than being dead. This edginess didn't fit her normal calm demeanor. She sulked about the room then stopped to stare out the window. Maybe it was because she was alone in Castle MacKinnon for the first time in months. She sighed, taking in the lack of a clear reflection in the glass.

Only a hazy outline appeared, but she knew what she looked like. Long, red hair dropped to her waist, which had always been a task to untangle. Bright-green eyes that Gavin claimed couldn't hide a lie if she tried would be staring back at her if she weren't a ghost. Absently, she brushed her hair from her eyes then laughed at her absurdity. In her spiritual form, even if the wind blew, her hair always remained perfect. What had Izzy said about that? Oh yeah. It was a trick most women would die for. She couldn't help but smile at the memory of that discussion.

Ever since Ericka freed Gavin and Izzy freed Ian from the curse, her spiritual existence had taken a more positive spin. No longer was she alone in her quest to free her *brathairs*. The castle was filled with voices and life again after years of solitude and silence. What seemed like eons had passed before her eldest *brathair* was freed. During those centuries, she'd protected Gavin until the woman he was destined to love crossed his path. Akira sighed. *Gaol*, love, played an important role in their freedom.

She floated from the window and settled her ghostly being on the settee near the empty fireplace. It matter not that no fire warmed the room. Neither cold nor heat normally affected her. Then why did it suddenly seem frigid to her?

A whoosh filled the room and she sat erect. Nothing appeared but she sensed something reached out to her. It weakly called her name, but she could not follow nor could she answer. Her deal with the angels bound her to the castle and immediate grounds until the last *brathair* was found. Then she'd seek her rest in the Garden of Angels and not one moment before.

Akira focused on the voice. It grew stronger. Since she could not leave, maybe *it* would find her if she concentrated on it. Seconds seemed long before a being formed in the room near the window. This was a first. In all her centuries of death, no one ever contacted her other than the angels who wanted to guide her over into the spirit world.

"Who are ye?" she questioned the fuzzy image of the other female ghost. "And what business do ye have at Castle MacKinnon?"

"I am Mary Campbell of Breadalbane, cousin of the Campbells of Glenorchy and I have come to seek council with Akira."

She eyed the other ghost suspiciously. "I am Akira MacDonell of Castle MacKinnon. How have ye found me?"

It appeared as if Mary was uncertain if she should speak. She glanced around the room then back to Akira. "May I speak in confidence?"

"Aye, it is safe. We are alone." Akira's curiosity rose.

"I found ye because we are bound by a common thread. Your husband gave something to my cousin to hide. Something I took a solemn oath to protect 'til it was deemed safe for his return."

If her heart still beat, Akira knew it would pound heavily at the moment. "Aye," she stated softly as she forced the word to form across the excited knot in her throat.

"Your *brathair*, Struan, has been found."

Instantly, Struan's riddle recited in Akira's head.

Thy mighty Ben Lawers surrounds thee

Four rounded forts protect thy sleeping bairn

Chained within the center floats thy fourth

Safe beneath thy watchful eye of Breadalbane

Rest ye weary one fer yer day of release shall come

Lest nay be the month of one when thy favored fish of Balloch run

Was Mary of Breadalbane the watchful eye? Considering Akira had chosen to linger in this world as Gavin's protector, maybe this Mary had done the same for Struan. Were they lovers? As women of 1740, it was not proper to discuss such matters. Being dead, Akira felt that trumped the late society's rules.

"Why did you protect my *brathair*? Why did you not cross over?"

Mary's chin tilted and a shy smile formed. "Honor and *gaol* bound me to your clan."

"You were in love with Struan?"

"Aye, but we never acted on our feelings." Mary shook her head sadly as she paused, then added, "I was betrothed to another. When my cousin died, I alone knew where Straun lay hidden and vowed to protect him even in death, which came sooner than anticipated. My husband poisoned me for not providing a male bairn."

Akira hugged Mary. "'Tis a sorry fate you received but I thank you for your sacrifice."

Mary pulled from the hug. "It was not easy. Though the angels took pity on the way I died, I had to bargain with them in order to protect Struan."

Akira laughed. "So did I. How is it you can travel when I am bound to MacKinnon land?"

"As I said," Mary replied. "We are tied by a common thread. Both protect the ones we loved within the same clan. I reached out to you but cannot reach out to any other. My travel is restricted to you and limited in time. I have but a wee few minutes to visit before I shall be returned home."

Suddenly something clicked inside Akira's thoughts. She protected Gavin. Izzy's mother lingered to watch over her little girl and thus protected Ian in the process. Mary protected Struan. All were women who chose to linger to protect a loved one or a MacKinnon *brathair*. Were there others like them? It warmed her cold, dead heart to know each of her *brathairs* may have a guardian assigned to watch over them.

"Where has Struan been found?" she asked.

Mary looked at Akira as if she warred with the decision to answer. "Loch Tay."

Akira floated over to the giant map that hung on the wall. She located Loch Tay and wished she could stick a bright-blue pin in it to show the others when they returned. She turned to look at Mary. "Who found him?"

"A woman named Caledonia."

"Caledonia," Akira repeated on a heavy sigh. "A strong, Scottish name. A woman given the proper name of Scotland should be perfect to save my *brathair*."

"He has already been saved. They lifted him from the bottom o' Loch Tay at dusk." Mary's perplexed look made Akira smile. The other ghost had no idea what they were dealing with in the form of this curse.

"Mary, he has simply been found. Not saved." Akira floated in a circle. "It is *gaol* which shall set him free."

"How?" Mary questioned.

"As you know, my *brathairs* were cursed into stone centuries ago by Hume MacGillivray. He hated my *brathair*, Gavin, for marrying Tavia. He issued the *Curse of the Gargoyle* against them and imprisoned them. The curse was not final. When he realized his mistake, he set out to find their statues and destroy them. That is why they were hidden. I was given an anti-curse with which to free them."

"And you didn't. Why?" The judgmental implication in Mary's tone irked Akira, but she stifled the anger and explained.

"It was a partial release. I could not in good conscience release them to suffer a half-life. Man by night and stone by day."

"Oooo," Mary sighed, sadness lacing her tone. "It is a horrid design to this curse."

"Aye, but there is a path to true freedom," Akira proclaimed with a smile. "*Gaol*, love."

"*Gaol*?" Mary's brows bunched and Akira read her confusion.

Akira placed her arm around Mary's shoulders. "*M'Caraid*, let me teach you the verse of the anti-curse with which you are to share with this Caledonia. You must teach her to speak it clearly in Gaelic for it to work."

"Will it save Struan from the curse?"

"It shall be a start," Akira claimed. "The rest lay in the hands of *gaol*. May his cold heart open for the arms of love."

Chapter Three

Caledonia cleaned the statue into the wee hours of the morning. Long after the others went to bed, she stayed and worked. Something inside her drove her to continue, until her arms ached and her hands cramped. She cupped the statue's cheek and stared at his eyes.

"Oh, if you were real," she whispered longingly.

Tired fingers traced his masculine jaw then dropped to linger on his chest, before absently trailing lower. His shirt was tucked neatly into the waistband of his kilt, which ended above his knee. A belt wrapped his narrow waist. What looked like a rabbit fur sporran hung at his right hip. Solid, muscled calves were visible and she bet if she lifted his kilt, matching thighs supported this gorgeous hunk.

Not to mention what she might find between them. She trembled at the thought. *Don't go there. You really are suffering from sleep deprivation if a statue's making you horny.* Caledonia stepped back but couldn't stop her seriously tired perusal of this masterpiece. She'd scrubbed every section of this creation and studied every nook and cranny. Nowhere on it did she find the artist's signature, a date, or any indication as to who posed for this statue.

Caledonia continued to linger in its presence, even though her body begged for bed. She shrugged off the tiredness for a moment longer as she circled the statue one more time, trailing her hand along its fine attributes. There were no visible flaws in this man's physique. Strong arms meant to protect. She palmed his biceps. Massive. Before she could stop herself, she fantasized about being wrapped in those arms. Warm. Safe. Protected.

She shook her head and glanced around to make sure no one witnessed her moment of insanity. Nope. What did she expect? It was three in the morning. No one else was even up at this ungodly hour. She took one last, long look at her prize then put her tools away. Dead tired, she locked the side door to the oversized shed they'd converted into the central station for the salvage business. Its location at the dock behind their family cottage made it convenient. She hesitated with her hand upon the outside handle.

Was he safe?

He? The statue! Was *it* safe? she silently reprimanded.

Normally she didn't think twice about leaving anything inside the salvage shed. Something sparked mistrust to skitter across her skin in the form of chills, which ended with the tiny hairs on the back of her neck standing on end. Caledonia tried to swallow the unsubstantiated sensation. No one stole in this village. Everyone knew everyone. They were one big, extended family. But Kip wasn't a part of the village and *he* was here. Would he steal from her?

Again.

Caledonia double-checked the lock as she tried to douse the flame of suspicion igniting in her gut. Not in her hometown. He wouldn't have the nerve to try anything.

Rubbing the back of her neck, she decided this line of thought wouldn't have occurred if she weren't so tired. Kip didn't have the balls to act against her, not with Able and Percy as her bodyguards. A smile upturned her lips and she noted the effort even that small action took. She walked the short distance across the yard, entered through the back door and painstakingly dragged her tired butt upstairs to her room.

The quick, hot shower did nothing to ease the ache of her strained muscles, but at least it removed the dirt and silt. Afterward, too tired to care or dress, she dropped face-first onto the bed, wrapped in an oversized towel. Images of him filled her brain. No matter how she tried, she couldn't stop thinking of the mystery man behind the statue. Was he a member of a royal family? What was his place in Scottish history? Was he kind, loving and passionate?

She bet those lips were tasty. And those hands... Umm, they probably knew how to touch and tease a woman to perfection. If the size of his hands were any indication, then the rest of him was probably built for pleasure as well.

Oh God, was she exhausted. Caledonia huffed, dragging the pillow from under the bedspread and tucking it beneath her head. Squeezing her eyes shut tight, she urged her thoughts to cease. She needed to rest and thinking of a hot Scottish laird who didn't exist got her nowhere. Instead it made her ache for something she couldn't have.

"Caledonia."

Her eyes opened wide, but she saw nothing but the bedding. Cautiously, Caledonia lifted and slowly turned to look in the direction of the voice. Beside her window stood the female ghost she swore she saw earlier on the *Marcail Struana*. She sat upright, rubbed her eyes, but the spirit remained. It didn't disappear.

The woman floated closer and coolness surrounded Caledonia to the point she wrapped the bedspread around her to fight the sudden chill. The woman stood small in size, had large, doe-like brown eyes that were striking in her petite, oval face. Her hair was quaffed in an ancient do that Caledonia knew from her studies meant she was a woman of privilege.

"I have come to give you a message."

"A message," Caledonia managed to sputter through dry lips. "Who are you?"

"I am Mary Campbell o' Breadalbane," she stated proudly with her chin tilted, giving Caledonia the impression she was considered an important person in her time. "You have found a lost MacKinnon *brathair*. It is up to you to free him from the curse."

Caledonia quickly darted a glance to the bed to see if she were actually still lying there and this was a strange dream. Nope, she wasn't having an out-of-body experience, so this must be real. She pinched herself and instantly knew she was awake. Staring at the ghost, she stumbled over her words.

"Whhhhaaat…" She cleared her throat and tried again. "Save who from what? I don't understand."

"Let me explain," the ghostly figure said.

It settled on the bed beside her as if they were two young girls at a slumber party and one was about to spill a secret. Coldness wafted off the spirit's form in waves. If she'd known company was coming she would've dressed proper for bed, instead of wearing nothing but a towel after her shower. Caledonia shuddered as she tucked the covers tighter around her against the chill. She did a double take to make sure nothing peeked out from beneath the bedspread.

Not that she was modest or shy. She couldn't count the number of times in her life she or the O'Reillys changed in front of one another, but she'd grown up with them. They were like her brothers. This ghost wasn't. From her appearance, Caledonia knew this spirit was old. If she had to guess from Mary's clothes, seventeenth or eighteenth century, maybe, but clothing fashion of the past wasn't her forte. Kip had handled dating items of that nature they found. She shook the unwanted image of him from her head and focused on Mary's ancient dialect. She didn't want to miss one word.

"Many years past, a curse was cast upon the *brathairs* o' Clan MacKinnon. It turned them into stone statues. For their safety, the *brathairs* were hidden so they could not be destroyed. You have found the *brathair*, Struan MacKinnon, fourth son o' Farlan MacKinnon."

"Fourth son," she repeated. Caledonia's eyes widened as another piece of the puzzle fell into place.

Chained within the center floats thy fourth

Was this fourth son of Farlan MacKinnon the fourth from the poem?

Safe beneath thy watchful Eye of Breadalbane

What did she say her name was? Mary Campbell of Breadalbane. Was she this watchful eye? This ghost. A forgotten image from her past shot to the forefront of her exhausted brain as recognition kicked into gear. Caledonia slid from the bed and spun to face this ghost, this Mary of Breadalbane.

"You were the one who screamed at us in the root cellar."

"Aye," Mary simply replied as if it were common knowledge. "It was my sworn oath to protect Struan. You stole the riddle."

"Riddle?" Caledonia's brow bunched. "It's not a poem?"

"Nay," Mary answered. "The *brathairs* were separated and given to different people in league with the MacKinnons to hide. My cousin accepted the responsibility but he took ill before he completed the task. I stepped into his place and upheld his oath o' sanctuary for Struan. Once he was hidden, we were obliged to provide clues on how to find him. It was me which chose his location and me which writ the riddle."

Caledonia paced. This had to be a dream. Her mind whirled. A curse. A *brathair*, which she knew from studying Gaelic meant brother. Brother. Brothers? She stopped and faced Mary, who still sat on her bed as if she belonged there.

"*Brathairs* as in plural?" When Mary gave her a confused look, she quickly added. "Was more than one *brathair* cursed?" She said the word but she wasn't sure if she believed it. A curse? Really?

"Aye." Mary nodded. "Clan MacKinnon was blessed with seven boys. All fell victim to this curse. One *piuthar,* sister, Akira survived and saved them from destruction."

"Seven brothers," Caledonia stated on a hushed breath as she plopped onto the bed beside Mary. "And this Struan was the fourth brother, umm, *brathair,*" she quickly corrected and used the Gaelic term so as not to add to Mary's confusion.

"Aye."

Caledonia stared at Mary. Disbelief warred with the incredible information this spectral being shared with her. This was a definite test of her faith in the other world. Time and time again, she'd fought with Kip over the fact spirits walked among them. She'd sworn to have seen them. Even heard them. But never had one sat beside her and held a conversation with her. Man, would Kip take back every mean word if he could see this. *He* was a true non-believer.

Was she truly a believer in the supernatural? Here sat the test of a lifetime. Caledonia studied Mary from head to toe. Though transparent, her overall appearance was that of a lady, prim and proper, perfectly dressed and not one hair out of place. The look in her green eyes touched Caledonia's heart.

Before she could stop herself, she said, "You were in love with him, weren't you? That's why you hid him."

Mary did the first nervous thing Caledonia saw her do. She bit the edge of her lower lip as if she contemplated her answer. The sight of a crystal-clear tear slid down the spirit's face then disappeared. No moisture hit the floor. No sign of wetness followed its path but Caledonia knew what she'd seen. The woman cried for the man she loved.

"Aye," she finally admitted on a soft sigh. "My heart belonged to Struan. But it was not meant to be."

"Did he love you?" For some reason she couldn't explain, Caledonia wanted to know.

"That is an answer I cannot give." Mary shook her head. "The words were never spoken. Struan was a respectable man. We honored an unspoken decision between us not to act upon the feelings we both sensed grew. It is the reason my heart aches."

Wow. Caledonia was floored. Here sat a woman of pure conviction and dedication. She obviously loved this Struan. If what she said was true, then she'd been protecting his hiding place for centuries and for what? Unrequited love? Words tumbled from her lips. "You did all this without knowing if he truly felt the same way? You never acted on your feelings. Why?"

"In my time, much was expected of a woman. We held no power, yet we were traded 'n' bartered between clans for better stations in society. A woman of my position chose no husband. He was chosen for you." Sadness tainted her tone and Caledonia swallowed hard against the lump in her throat. She had no choice. That was unfair. But that was how it was. Caledonia gritted her teeth at the injustice of the era.

"*Gaol* is a powerful ruler of the soul. When you find it, peace will follow. I let the pressures of my family rule my decision and did not follow my heart. It was a wrong that cost my life. That is why the angels let me linger to protect Struan." Mary touched Caledonia in the center of her chest. Ice cold shot through her but she didn't flinch. Something in Mary's eyes made her sit still and listen as she continued. "You must learn the anti-curse. You must speak it clearly. It is up to you to set him free."

* * * * *

Bright light shone through the window. Caledonia woke with a start. She sat upright, rubbing her eyes. When the clock came into view, she stopped mid-stretch. Nine o'clock. Oh God, she'd overslept. Never had she slept this late. Not since she was a teen. Caledonia flipped the covers off. Something went flying across the room. Her notebook hit the wall with a thud then slid to the floor.

When she picked it up, she froze. Written in her handwriting were words in Gaelic. Some she recognized. Others she didn't. As she straightened, she read the verse.

Ceum saor de clach
Be Ye Biast air duine
Tis Gaol dara slighe

Ge Ye be mèinne
Dh'oidche mur dh'là

What the… Caledonia's knees gave way and she sank onto the foot of her bed. It wasn't a dream. Mary truly visited and spoke with her. Here on this page sat the proof. She could've sworn it was a bizarre, complicated dream brought on by sheer exhaustion.

Maybe she walked in her sleep and wrote this then. After all, she was overly tired when she went to bed last night. Anything was possible. She desperately tried to convince herself, but knew the truth. Mary Campbell of Breadalbane visited her from the spirit world and gave her a mission.

Save Struan MacKinnon from the curse.

Was there really a curse? Was any of this real? Caledonia sighed heavily as she stared at the words in her hand. She shook her head. What if this was a curse? What if a man was entombed in a statue by said curse? What if he would come to life if she simply stated these words as Mary claimed?

What if? That's what her life had boiled down to… A bunch of *what ifs*.

Caledonia stood, grabbed the robe off the back of her door and slipped it on. She sat at her desk with the notepad and her laptop. After logging on, she located a Gaelic-English dictionary. It didn't take her long to translate the verse.

Step free of stone

Be you beast or man

It is love either way

Though you be mine

By night if not by day

Cute. It translated into a nonsensical verse. If she spoke these words would he be free? From the first line, it seemed that was the case. The second line confused her. Beast or man? What did that mean? After all these years, could he have turned into some sort of beast? Nah, it didn't compute. If he was cursed as a man it led one to believe he'd remain a man. *If curses were real.* She sighed as a smidgeon of doubt filtered into her thoughts. Did she truly believe this?

Caledonia read the next line. What did love have to do with this? Thinking about it, love had a lot to do with it. Mary lingered, caught between heaven and Earth because of her unwavering love for Struan. Mary didn't know if he felt the same for her. According to her, he never actually spoke the words. In her heart, she believed he did. Caledonia leaned back in her chair.

What would it be like to experience a love like what Mary felt for Struan? She closed her eyes and tried to visualize anyone who'd love her strongly enough to beg the angels to let their spirit remain to guard her cursed and trapped soul for all eternity—or until someone found her and set her free, whichever came first. She opened her eyes and knew only her parents loved her like that.

A tap on her door snapped her from her thoughts.

"Caledonia, are you well?" The sweet lilt of her mother's brogue filtered through the door.

"Aye," Caledonia replied as she opened the door. "I overslept."

"Nay, you didn't oversleep. I heard the shower and know you didn't stop working until the wee hours of the morning. Your body needed the rest so it took it." She walked into the room with a tray resting on her hip. She set it down on the desk. "I made your breakfast. Your poppa's already down at the shed. He said not to wake you. So I didn't. I waited to hear you moving about before I came up."

Caledonia couldn't help but smile. Her parents had the best relationship. It's what she wanted and thought she had when she married Kip. The image of him chased the smile from her lips so she quickly lifted the teacup and blew across its rim. No need for Momma to see her smile disappear. Any discussion of Kip always upset Momma and that was the last thing Caledonia wanted.

A soft mew and the brush of fur against her ankle made her almost snort tea through her nose. Even before she looked down, she knew the source. She set her cup on the desk and scooped up the tiny gray kitten. It had the oddest jet-black stripe running from the bridge of its nose down its back to the tip of its tail, giving it a distinctive appearance.

"I see we've gained another stray to the brood," Caledonia said as she stroked the velvet-soft kitten. Big blue eyes stared at her while it attached its claws to her robe as if it were afraid Caledonia would drop her.

"Not a stray," Momma proclaimed proudly as she detached the kitten from Caledonia's robe. She took it and snuggled it close. Extreme joy showed on her face. "Tabby had a litter. We now have five new additions to our brood. You're going to love the little buggers when you see them."

"So that's where she went." It was good to know Tabby had returned safely. She'd become the family pet and when she disappeared for a few weeks, Momma was heartbroken. Seeing her with this new kitten made Caledonia's smile return because she knew it healed Momma's heart.

Tabby was near death when she landed on the stoop about a year ago, and didn't leave like the others once they were well. Momma never turned away a stray animal, especially an injured one. It didn't matter that they lived on a tight budget. She somehow managed to make ends meet, fed the stragglers and healed whatever illness the animal might have when it showed up. That was Momma, tenderhearted and loving.

Caledonia plopped into her chair. Did Momma believe in curses? She was the one who enlightened Caledonia to the fact spirits walked among them. She taught her to recognize the signs that a spirit may be near. A chill in the air when there was otherwise none, a scent or fragrance that seemed out of place or a faint vision of a person in the form of a shadow or transparent figure. If anyone could help with this, it would be Momma.

"What's your opinion of curses?"

Momma's brows bunched as she carefully stroked the kitten. "As in the use of naughty language or in the form of a spell?"

"A spell," Caledonia clarified.

Aileen Kavanagh set the kitten on the floor, picked up the hairbrush and began the task of untangling Caledonia's hair as if she were still a child. Caledonia didn't stop her. She liked it. It not only helped relax her, it made her momma happy by doing it.

"As I understand, curses are a form of black magic. They are not to be used lightly."

"Then you believe in them?"

"I believe there are many things in this world that are unexplainable. They just happen without a valid reason behind them." Momma tugged her hair into three separate sections to braid. "Remember what happened when you tried to dive in that triangle. You believed that place to be cursed. From what you told me, I never doubted your theory for a second."

Her lungs tightened at the memory. Never had anything scared her as badly as that dive. It almost made her quit the salvage business. Every piece of her equipment stopped working the moment she slipped under the surface of the warm Bermuda waters. No air reached her lungs. The water weighed her down. Invisible hands grabbed hold and tugged her toward the bottom. In a battle that seemed like hours, she struggled for the surface only to find out she'd been submerged for mere seconds.

A thorough inspection of the diving equipment showed no evidence of damage or improper function. That was proof enough to her the waters were cursed. She refused to dive again and that initiated the first of many disputes with

Kip. They canned the expedition because if she wasn't comfortable with a dive, the O'Reilly boys supported her decision and no one dove.

Momma's hand cupped her chin, tilting her face upward. "What's got you thinking on curses? Was it the spirit visitor you had last night?"

Caledonia shouldn't be surprised, but she was just a little bit. "You knew?"

"Aye. I felt a presence in the air. Who came to visit?"

"A woman named Mary Campbell of Breadalbane. Have you ever heard of her haunting this area?" Caledonia turned and watched Momma as she lifted the kitten and settled it onto her lap when she sat on the bed.

"Mary," she repeated softly.

Aileen's brows pursed as she shuffled through her thoughts. Caledonia liked the way her forehead crinkled when she tried to recall a memory buried deep in her vault of tales. As a child, her momma shared many stories and tales of Scottish lore and myths at bedtime. Caledonia took a sip of her tea. Maybe that's why she traveled the globe in search of treasure. She'd had a great dose of fantasy, romanticism and adventure instilled in her soul from day one.

Her blue eyes brightened when her gaze leveled on Caledonia. "When I was a lass, my grandma told me a tale of a young woman named Mary, who once lived in the castle on the north end of the loch. She was bound in a loveless marriage, which bore no children. She died young, spurring rumors of poison at the hand of her husband for the lack of an heir. It's been said her ghost could be seen on occasion standing at the water's edge as if waiting for a lover's return."

"She is the very same," Caledonia replied. "She explained her death and why she walks this world instead of crossing over."

"She mourns a lover," Momma stated with heavy anticipation in her tone. Always the romantic, Caledonia noted about her mother.

"Aye, there is some truth to the tale." Caledonia paused. If anyone would believe what Mary shared with her, it was Momma. "Her husband did poison her because of no heir. But she doesn't mourn a lover. She lingered to protect one. The man she loves fell victim to a curse, which turned him to stone."

Her eyes widened. "The statue."

"The statue." Caledonia nodded.

Chapter Four

She stood outside the open doorway, looking in. The double doors, which faced the dock, were both opened wide, filling the main room with light. The sight of the statue in the morning sun gave her the chills. A glorious warrior stood proudly, ready for battle with his hand upon his sword. She soaked in the beauty of the greatest find of her life. A centuries-old artifact, but did it hold a secret? Inside that solid wall of stone was there really a cursed soul waiting for release?

The way the sun brushed across his face gave him a strikingly handsome appeal. The eyes seemed to stare straight at her, which made her uncomfortable. But not enough so that she looked away. She couldn't. The surprised sadness she read within them burrowed into her heart. If the words Mary spoke were true, a man lay trapped within this cocoon of stone.

"Morning, lass. Did you get your rest?" Poppa's voice sounded as if it came from the statue. It was all she could do not to jump. She didn't see him until he peeked from behind it.

She quickly cleared her throat and shook off the slight start he had inadvertently given her. "Morning, Poppa." Caledonia moved to his side and kissed his cheek. "Aye, more than I needed."

"Nay, you needed it." He held an unlit cigar between his fingers and a cleaning rag in the other hand. Caledonia snorted at the sight. He'd given up smoking several years prior to appease Momma, but he claimed he kept cigars handy to chew on the ends and pretend. That was their little secret. She liked the way his short, gray hair shimmered in the morning sun and his blue eyes held a twinkle in them that hinted he was up to mischief. And he was with that cigar in his hand. Caledonia grinned. If Momma caught him…

The back screen door flapped closed and echoed across the yard. Neither had to look to know who headed their way. The scent of fresh scones wafted on the breeze announcing Momma's approach. Poppa tucked the cigar into a side pocket of his coveralls. Percy and Able hurried up the dock, carrying a large bucket of water from the loch between them. It was an everyday practice they did for Aileen. She used it to water her garden.

"Thank you, boys," Aileen said as they set the bucket in its normal spot behind the shed. When she rounded the shed, she stopped beside Caledonia. "So this is the statue."

"Aye, it is," Fin Kavanagh replied, and then moved to kiss her cheek and acquired a scone in the process. After a bite, he proclaimed, "Ummm, delicious, just like the woman who made them."

Aileen's cheeks flushed red. Her gaze never left Poppa's. Percy didn't miss the chance to poke a jib at her poppa like always. The camaraderie between him and the O'Reillys was better than most fathers and sons.

"Don't be telling me that sort o' dribble works on the ladies," Percy taunted with a wink at Aileen Kavanagh.

"If'n you and your brother learned a wee bit o' dribble, maybe you'd be as lucky as me and you wouldn't still be living in your mother's house and sleeping alone."

"Oh that hurts, Mr. Kavanagh," Able chimed in as he covered his heart with his hand and pretended offense.

"And who says we're sleeping alone?" Percy teased.

"Still sharing a bed with your brother, are you?" Fin quipped without missing a beat and Caledonia burst out laughing.

"Hey, you're supposed to be on our side." Able shot a mock frown her way.

Waving her hands in front of her, she laughingly begged, "Leave me out of this one."

"I set the kettle on before I came down here. What say you men continue this discussion in the kitchen over tea?"

Aileen suggested. When they agreed, she gave a knowing nod to Caledonia and walked away.

Their playful argument continued as they strolled across the backyard, following Aileen and her plate of scones to the house for tea.

Alone with Struan.

She sighed and stepped back. When had she started thinking of the statue as Struan? That's what Mary called him, Struan, and it must've stuck in her head, she decided. She fumbled with the folded paper she tugged from the back pocket of her jeans. Thanks to Mary, she felt she knew the pronunciations well enough to speak the anti-curse. Lord knows Mary's persistence wouldn't let her rest until she'd gotten it right last night. No wonder she'd slept so late.

Caledonia peeked around the corner of the shed toward the house. The men were safely occupied inside, thanks to Momma. Her fresh-baked scones were the perfect ruse to draw them into the house for tea. It had been her plan all along so Caledonia would have private access in order to complete her task uninterrupted.

She swallowed, trying to quell the nerves crawling up her spine, which threatened to take over her vocal cords and prevent her from speech. A nervous laugh escaped. What if she got it wrong? Caledonia paced around the solid stone being. A strange tingling bloomed in the pit of her stomach and blossomed to spread across her abdomen and then stretched upward.

She licked her lips, took a breath then spoke in as steady and as clear a voice as she could. *"Ceum saor de clach. Be ye biast air duine. Tis gaol dara slighe. Ge ye be mèinne. Dh'oidche mur dh'là."*

Nothing happened. Was it supposed to be instantaneous? Caledonia rolled her eyes. That was one thing she'd forgotten to ask. How long would it take for the anti-curse to work?

"It will be the fall o' night before you see his handsome face."

Caledonia turned to see Mary hovered inside the shed directly behind Struan's statue. "Why nightfall?"

"It is the way o' the Curse of the Gargoyle. Man by night. Stone by day."

That explained *though ye be mine by night if not by day*—sort of. Curse of the Gargoyle. Weren't those mythical creatures that were stone by day and alive at night? She made a mental note to check that later. Gargoyles weren't exactly on the top of her list of important things to study, so she didn't know much about them, if anything.

"Are you sure it worked?" Caledonia whispered, stepping inside the shed, closing the distance between them.

"Nay," Mary stated as she shook her head. "We shall see come nightfall."

The back screen door slammed, causing Caledonia to jump. Mary vanished. Male voices sounded and got louder as they moved closer. Great. She sat on a stool and stared at the statue. This was going to be the longest day of her life.

* * * * *

Through binoculars, he watched. She acted oddly the moment the men went into the house. It didn't matter. She was probably overly excited about her success. When the double doors facing the dock opened, the view of her prize was spectacular from his position opposite the loch.

From this distance, it wasn't easily discernable as to the era from which the statue came. It appeared to be some sort of Scotsman, which made sense. She did retrieve it from a Scottish loch. Who was it supposed to be? Had she stumbled upon a sculpture of a famous Scottish warrior, like Rob Roy or maybe William Wallace? Wouldn't that be grand? he mused.

If it turned out to be one of them, then its value would double. Maybe even triple. He let the binoculars drop to hang around his neck. Now that he knew what she'd found, all he needed was a buyer. Taking it from her wouldn't be hard, considering where she stored it. A shed in the backyard of her parents' home didn't exactly equal a high-security vault.

* * * * *

For once in her life, she was right. The day dragged. Every time she thought she heard something odd, like a creak or a snap, she studied the statue for a crack. To the others, her actions must've seemed strange, but none commented if they noticed. She tried to remain calm, but she couldn't. She'd spoken the words and the closer it got to nightfall, her heartbeat increased and anticipation captured her imagination.

Was this real? In the afternoon, she'd taken the time to read up on the gargoyle legends. Most were guardians of man. Some were evil, while others remained neutral. But all suffered the same fate at sunrise. No matter where they were or what they were doing, they turned to stone.

Would that be Struan's fate? Would he return to stone every day at sunrise?

Caledonia paced the dock. When had she accepted this curse as truth? She snorted. She knew when. Between the appearance of Mary, her convincing story and Momma's beliefs that anything unexplainable was possible, she'd been suckered into this mystical realm of distorted magic. She stared out over the loch.

In the distance she saw two fishing boats bobbing on the water. She knew her parents were in one of those boats, spending the late afternoon into the early evening, spinning tales and drowning bait with some of their lifelong pals. Poppa always said Momma was a true one-of-a-kind when he met her. On their first date, they went fishing and still routinely fished the loch together.

Caledonia knew her mother planned this sudden fishing afternoon to get Poppa out of the way. In case the curse were true, Aileen had whispered to her right before they left. She also knew the tradition of their fishing jaunts ended by docking at the Thistle Pub for drinks and dinner.

Those two wouldn't be back until long after the sun went down.

A half smile twisted her lips as she shook her head and released a soft sigh. It was good to be home, doing what she enjoyed with the people she loved. She turned on her heel and couldn't help but level her gaze on the statue. From where she stood, it looked like a heap of stone, its features undistinguishable in the growing shadows of the fading day.

Earlier, after the final cleaning of the statue, the men took the afternoon off and left her alone. Poppa and the O'Reillys hadn't understood her desire to wait a day or two before contacting the press. But they'd respected her wishes. Hell, she didn't even understand why she held off. If she were Kip…

She hugged herself tight against that thought, knowing she wasn't like Kip. He'd have plastered his find on the antiquities websites, notified an auction house and scoured the world for the highest bidder. Finding relics was a joy to be shared as a part of history, not hidden in some rich man's collection. Caledonia shivered though there was no wind.

"It is almost time." Mary's whisper came across her right shoulder and made her jump. She should've known the spirit was near when she felt a chill and shivered. But she'd been preoccupied. She shook Kip from her thoughts and faced Mary.

Through the spirit's transparency, she saw the sun sink low on the horizon. She was an eerily beautiful picture, a vision from the past in all her elegance highlighted by the vibrant colors of the fading sun. Caledonia simply stared. Soon the last rays of light would disappear and they would learn if she'd spoken the anti-curse correctly. *If* such an event should happen. Caledonia released a heavy breath and turned to walk to the shed.

"No reason for anyone to see this," Caledonia said as she grabbed one of the large doors to close it. *If anything actually happened.* Doubt taunted her system and chilled the blood in her veins. What if she'd wasted a day because of some spirit with a misguided conception of love?

After she closed the other door, Caledonia switched on the lights just as the last stream of sunlight disappeared. Seconds passed and nothing happened.

"Say it again," Mary whispered. Caledonia couldn't believe she was doing this. Nothing happened. It was just a statue, not a cursed man. Seeing the anxious look in Mary's eyes, Caledonia cleared her throat and tried again just to appease a ghost.

"Ceum saor de clach. Be ye biast air duine. Tis gaol dara slighe. Ge ye be mèinne. Dh'oidche mur dh'là."

The last word barely left her lips when the floor shook, causing her to step backward. A low rumble reverberated from the statue. A sizzle hissed through the air and static electricity lifted the few loose strands of hair from her braid. The heat level rose around her, but she refused to budge. Instead, she regained her balance and closed the short distance between her and the rock. Without checking, she knew Mary's eyes were locked on the statue.

A huge crack appeared. Bright light shot from the inside and she used her forearm as a shield and squinted. The statue shattered and crumbled into pieces at her feet, leaving behind a very disoriented man. Her jaw dropped and her eyes widened as she lowered her arm to her side. This couldn't have happened. Before she moved, angered words spoken on a thick Scottish brogue in ancient Gaelic heated her cheeks as he sprang at her.

His momentum shoved her back against the wall with him pressed tight against her. A solid man of muscle held her pinned as he rapidly made demands in a tongue she couldn't quite understand.

"Just slow down," she gasped. He held her by the neck with one massive hand and his face leveled with hers. She refused to back down though he intimidated the hell out of her. Keeping her wits about her, she took as much of a breath as his grip allowed and decided to speak in a tongue similar to Mary's. "You have to slow your speech. My Gaelic is rusty." She prayed he understood, even though she lied about knowing much of the Gaelic tongue.

His brows furrowed and his grip loosened. At first she took this as a good sign until he did the unexpected. His hand shifted to cup the back of her head and his lips captured her mouth in a rough, demanding kiss. It happened so quickly, she had no time to think. She simply reacted. Everything the O'Reillys taught her took over.

Right knee, swift and hard to the balls, followed by a solid jab to the ribs caused her assailant to crumble into a heap. He gasped for air, trying to cup his jewels with one hand, while holding his side with the other. She jumped over him and stood beside Mary, who wrapped a transparent arm around her waist as if she could tug her into a protective hug.

"What did you say?" Mary's puzzled gaze met hers and all she could do was shrug. She didn't know what she'd said that sufficed such a reaction. She placed a gap between her and Mary to ward off the chill being so close to the spirit caused. Her nipples hardened to sharp points and she didn't want the giant brute to get the wrong impression, so she hid them beneath crossed arms over her chest.

Carefully, she tested her battered lips with the tip of her tongue. His flavor teased her taste buds and ignited a hunger for more, which shocked her. Never had anyone kissed her so roughly. True, he'd shoved her against the wall, but instead of invoking fear, she noted she liked it and wanted more. Oh God, what was wrong with her? Caledonia closed her eyes, momentarily sealing off the vision of the gorgeous hunk slumped on his knees.

Mary's voice caused Caledonia to focus on his every move. If he so much as lunged at the tender spirit, she'd... Well, she wasn't exactly sure what she'd do but she'd do something. Even though she didn't think he could actually hurt a ghost if he attacked her.

Crouched on the floor, he took a moment to regroup. *Och*, the *boireannach*, woman, grounded him with a sharp knee to his baws. Sucking a breath between clenched teeth, he cupped himself and scouted his surroundings through lowered lids. Nothing familiar came into sight. Slow, deliberate movements of his head from one side to the other garnered him a limited visual, but he sensed only the *boireannach* stood behind him and nay one else.

He'd awoken in a place other than home. Had he been taken captive? Where was he? Where were his *brathairs*, his family? What happened to MacGillivray? There was no doubt the mongrel was behind this plot. Anger mixed with confusion as he tried to clear his head. A rich, feminine scent teased his senses, reminding him of his mistake. Why had he kissed the *boireannach* without her permission? Never had he taken what was not willingly given. He tasted her on his lips, a fine blend of feisty Scottish lass and honey.

Struan tilted his head ever so slightly. An odd light shone in the ceiling. His breath hitched. A witch's magic. How had he come to be in a witch's hut? One face appeared within his mind's eye. MacGillivray. Where was the coward who conspired with a witch against the MacKinnons? It was the only answer as to how he had fallen without so much as a solid blow to MacGillivray's jaw. That was to be corrected the moment Struan found him. His free hand fisted at the ready. MacGillivray must answer for what he had done.

With each slight movement, his bawls reminded him of the woman who rendered him to his knees. If'n things were different, he would show her how quickly a MacKinnon recovered and teach her the joy of his touch. *Och*, but things were not that way. Desperate need to find MacGillivray and protect his family pumped through his veins. He palmed the sword's hilt and prepared to take his stand.

Fight or die. Either way it was better than being a prisoner. Struan took stock of his position, ignored the throb between his thighs and prepared to do battle for his freedom and that of his family.

"Struan MacKinnon." The tender use of his name struck a chord of familiarity and his grip eased upon the hilt, but did not release it. *Mary.* Slowly he rose to his feet, daring glances from side to side, searching for the gentle beauty.

"Struan MacKinnon." Again Mary stated his name and Caledonia heard the admiration and love in her lilt, yet her tone held a commanding air.

Caledonia watched for any signs the man heard Mary. If she blinked, she would have missed his subtle movements. With the fluid grace of a vested warrior, he stood. When he turned, Mary floated in front of him. He stepped back. His pallor drained as he gasped.

"Mary, you are a spirit." He pointed at Caledonia. "It is the work of a witch."

"Aye, I am a spirit, through no hand of a witch. Nay, Caledonia is not a witch." She nodded then smiled. "You have been entombed in stone by a curse for over two hundred years, *M'Gaol.*"

"A curse…" It was the only answer. "He would not have captured me 'n a fair fight." Struan growled, took a step then suddenly stopped. His eyes closed tight and his expression showed extreme pain. Caledonia attempted to help him, but the shake of Mary's head stilled her movements.

As if the past replayed behind his eyes, Struan roared in anger. A warrior's mask shifted his face into a macabre appearance of sheer hatred. In a solid, swift stroke, the Claymore left the sheath at his side and he swirled about in a predatory stance on the hunt for prey. His words seethed with deadly intent on a horrific bellow.

"MacGillivray. Where are you, you bastard?"

When his gaze leveled on Caledonia, Mary floated between them as if she could shield Caledonia if he chose to attack. Her chin lifted and the spirit's shoulders squared as she delivered her news.

"He is dead."

"Dead." The massive man's shoulders lowered, but his sword didn't waver. It remained readied for battle. His brows bunched and his jaw tightened as if he contemplated whether she spoke the truth or not.

"Aye, dead," Mary repeated.

"My family?" His tone softened but his battle stance didn't. The warrior's gaze never left Mary.

"Your *brathairs* fell to the curse same as you. Two have been freed. The others remain lost, for now."

The pain in his eyes tore at Caledonia's heart. Sheer love shone in those deep-sea blues. A love for family. Caledonia swallowed against the threat of tears.

After a moment, he found his voice again and asked, "And Akira? What be her fate?"

"She lingers such as I protecting those we *gaol*." She floated closer and brushed a transparent hand along his cheek. If he felt the chill, he didn't show it. Caledonia chewed the edge of her lip, nervously watching and wishing this sad scenario were simply a dream.

Pain and confusion wafted off the man in waves, attacking her sense of caring, pushing her to want to soothe his anguish. No words formed in her throat. Nothing came to mind that didn't sound contrite inside her head. What did you say to a two-hundred-plus-year-old Scottish laird who woke to a strange world and learned the fate of his family was not a desired one? She chose to remain still, watch and listen, hoping to learn a way to ease his discomfort without ending up on the sharp end of that Claymore.

"*M'Gaol*," he stated on a hushed breath. He sheathed his sword. When he attempted to touch her cheek, his hand penetrated her head and he jerked it back to his chest. Caledonia's heart hurt at the sight of pure, anguished surprise upon his face. All he wanted was to touch Mary and even that had been taken from him. The lump in Caledonia's throat grew.

"*M'Gaol*," Mary repeated then smiled. For several long seconds, they stared longingly at one another as if it finally sank in that they'd admitted their love for one another. But it was too late. No matter how hard she swallowed or sniffed, Caledonia couldn't have stopped the slow slide of tears this time.

"Your *brathairs*, Gavin and Ian, can be found along with Akira's spirit at Castle MacKinnon. It is a time where thy tongue is no longer Gaelic. It is English," Mary continued. Mary cupped his cheek and he closed his eyes as if relishing her touch, though Caledonia doubted he actually felt anything other than sheer cold upon his flesh. "*M'Gaol*, with your release comes mine. I leave you in safe hands." She looked over her shoulder. "Caledonia's."

She turned then floated closer. Mary touched Caledonia's cheek and proved her right in her thoughts. Icy coldness skittered across her flesh all the way to her toes, but she refused to visibly shiver. Instead, she met Mary's gaze. If she read it right, the ghost appeared relaxed, at peace.

She leaned in close to Caledonia's ear and whispered, "Take care of him. He deserves a second chance at love."

Mary's chin tilted heavenward and she nodded as if she answered someone's silent call. She returned to Struan then placed a kiss upon his cheek. A bright flash of light occurred and cold mixed with hot in the air around them. Mary disappeared, leaving behind a show of stars that sparkled a multitude of colors then dimmed into nothingness.

"She's crossed over," Caledonia stated in awe.

This was something she'd never forget. She witnessed one of the most beautiful love scenes ever. A woman lingered for centuries as a ghost, protected the man she loved, not knowing the truth until the very end. Mary went to the Garden of Angels with the knowledge her sacrifice was not wasted. He loved her as well, which set her soul at peace. Caledonia swore she saw that in Mary's eyes the moment before she crossed over.

Mary's whispered words filtered through her head. *"Kiss him, Caledonia. Make him yours and love him as well as I did and more."*

Caledonia took several steps toward Struan, uncertain if she should follow Mary's wishes. He looked befuddled by the whole thing. Yet, for some unexplainable reason, Mary's words refused to dissipate. It was as if the ghost controlled her actions. She grabbed him by the back of his neck and jerked him down to kissable level. Without giving him a chance, she planted a hot, plundering kiss. His mouth parted and she didn't hesitate to sample his flavor. Masculine and seductive. Caledonia commanded this kiss in much the same manner as he had their first—just not as brutal.

As fast as it started, she ended it. Out of breath and wanting more, she managed to place a gap between them. She released her grip and met his confused stare. Caught up in the moment, she poked his muscle-ripped chest with her forefinger as she spoke.

"*That's* how I like to be kissed. Not too hard, but not too soft either. Don't you forget it."

Pure laughter broke from him. Caledonia stepped back and simply stared. Did he not understand what she said? Or was he making fun of her? When he finally stopped, he cleared his throat, looked her straight in the eyes, and lowered so close to her face she felt the heat of his breath on her cheek.

"Lass." His thick brogue rolled on a deep timbre. "You got the drop on me this time. Be warned." He brushed his thumb across her bottom lip as he held her wide-eyed stare. "I won't be forgetting how you likes it."

He wasn't exactly sure where he was but one thing he did know—the black-headed minx with the oddest colored blue eyes he'd ever seen knew how to kiss. Pressed against her moments earlier stirred his blood back to life and hardened his shaft. Just the thought of it made him remember something else just as important if not more about this feisty *boireannach*. She knew how to bring a man to his knees and not in a pleasurable way. Absently, he shifted his stance, adjusting the injured party into a more comfortable position.

Taking in his surroundings more clearly, he still didn't recognize the room in which he stood. Odd items hung on the wall, lined the shelves and sat upon the table. He closed his eyes as his thoughts knotted. What had Mary said? Over two hundred years cursed. Gavin and Ian were freed, yet the others remained lost. Castle MacKinnon. Home.

He opened his eyes and leveled his gaze on the woman named Caledonia. Fine name for a strong woman. Studying her from head to toe, he deemed her different. On her bottom, she wore men's *trews* and some sort of shirt covered her upper half. Both items fit snug and reminded him she had fine curves.

Caledonia spoke. Her Scottish lilt tickled his ears. At least he woke in Scotland. Thank the angels. "My name is Caledonia Kavanagh."

"Milady." He nodded politely then replied, "I am Struan MacKinnon o' Clan MacKinnon from Lochsbury. Is what Mary said the truth? Have I been cursed for over two hundred years?"

"Aye," Caledonia replied.

He liked the way she met his gaze directly when she spoke. She didn't lower her eyes or play shy like the women of his time. Mary's image graced his thoughts and weighed heavy on his heart. Now there was a fine woman to whom he owed his life. He sighed, knowing that was a love that was never meant to be. He managed to find his voice and asked, "Where am I now?"

"Lawers Glen on the southern shore of Loch Tay."

He released a sigh of relief. He may not have woken in a familiar time, but he knew where he was. If he left right now, it would be several days walk for home. Struan turned for the door and was out of it before she could stop him.

"You mustn't go out there." Her voice followed behind him as did her footsteps.

Darkness surrounded him. A full moon hung over the loch, dancing across its surface. He inhaled deep. Fresh air filled his lungs. Freedom flowed through his veins. Though he tried to grapple with the knowledge, it seemed impossible over two hundred years had passed. The loch remained the same. He strolled down the dock. A large, strange-looking boat was moored alongside. A thick odor lingered near the rear of the boat and made his nose crinkle. It didn't smell natural.

The light of the moon granted him the ability to read the words written upon the boat's bow. *Marcail Struana.* Gaelic for pearl of the stream. It struck him odd to find such on this boat. His name *Struan* and the word *Struana* both meant stream. Was it coincidence or destiny he awakened in the care of this woman named Caledonia? Did she love the water in the same manner as he? Struan snorted at the thought as he continued past to the dock's end. Being frozen in stone muddled his brains with feminine thoughts of destiny.

If it were not for MacGillivray, his life would have remained in his time where he would have lived and died. Destiny. He shook his head but didn't prevent his gaze from lingering on the words written on the boat's bow. A mad man caused this havoc, not destiny. He stood on the very end of the dock, looking out across the water.

Odd lights twinkled along the shoreline in the night. Unfamiliar sounds cut the air. A low rumble. A distinctive hum. What made such noises? He squinted but only noted several sets of lights moving on the opposite side of the loch, as if they followed one another at a steady pace. His hand readied on his sword's hilt in case they somehow traversed the loch on a magical source. Was this world filled with such? Witch's magic?

He closed his eyes and struggled to wrap his mind around that issue. One moment he faced Hume MacGillivray, the next he stood beside a dark-haired beauty centuries later. How had he come to be at Loch Tay? Struan strained to remember.

He'd dressed and descended the stairs to await his brothers, Gavin and Ian, for an early-morning hunt. The great room was empty when he arrived. Gavin had a wife and a good reason to linger in bed, but Ian had none that would rescue him from Struan's wrath for being remiss in arriving on time. Footsteps echoed behind him. He turned expecting a *brathair*. Instead, he got an unwelcomed surprise.

In the garb of a monk, Hume MacGillivray stood with a black book opened in hand. Struan's demand to know why he foolishly chose to step foot on MacKinnon soil garnered a mumbled mystical response. He thought the man to be daft in the head. His attempt to draw his sword ended abruptly when his arms stilled. The air heated and snapped around him. A bright light engulfed him and darkness swallowed him. That was the last retrievable memory. MacGillivray's chant haunted his ears to the point he stiffened.

Struan balled and unballed his fists, then shifted his stance to prove to himself it was simply a horrific memory. He was free. But free to what, where and when? Mary was gone. His *brathairs* were cursed and he… Struan struggled to clear his thoughts. He wasn't sure about anything other than the fact he stood at the end of a dock trapped in a world he did not understand.

The touch of her hand on his forearm made him suddenly aware of her presence at his side. He looked at her. Streams of moonlight accentuated her face and gave her cerulean eyes a sensual, darker hue. A gentle breeze fluttered the strands that escaped her braid to lift and tease him with the urge to free the rest. It had been many a year since he'd seen such a beautiful woman. *Two hundred plus to be exact.* He squeezed his eyes shut against that thought as he desperately tried to accept it as fact.

"There have been many changes, Struan. Let me help you find your way." Her soft-spoken words touched him with her offer of guidance.

When he opened his eyes, Caledonia's reassuring gaze warmed his heart and stirred his blood, sending it directly to his shaft. *Mary said she left him in good hands. She basically gave him her blessing.* Struan heard the inner whisperings of the devilish voice inside his head. Here at his side stood an inviting woman who tempted him beyond belief. But he would not falter. An honorable man mourned the woman he loved and though they never even kissed, he'd loved Mary. Thoughts of lust be damned, he screamed inwardly. He knew nothing of Caledonia except the taste of her scrumptious mouth.

Struan tore his gaze away from Caledonia's full lips to stare across the loch. The thoughts that divided his mind at the moment confused him. Having been cursed for so long had to be the reason for this inner turmoil. It had to be the instigator behind this growing urge to couple with Caledonia. The cup of her hand to his cheek didn't help his situation. He followed the gentle pull of her touch and met her questioning gaze.

"Struan, I know this is all so difficult for you." He liked the way his name rolled on her lilt. She paused and he couldn't take his eyes off the tip of her tongue as she wet her lips. "I'm not even sure if I understand it myself. You've been in some sort of cursed state for a long time. You've got to be hungry. Let's go inside and I'll fix you a bowl of stew."

"Lass, food is not at the top of my needs at the moment." Struan steeled his resolve against the charms of the beauty he longed to touch as he said, "But it will satisfy my hunger in the only way I can allow."

Chapter Five

Caledonia wasn't sure what he meant about food not being his top need at the moment. But she knew she had to get him inside before someone saw him. She wasn't prepared to answer questions about who he was or where he came from. Hell, she wasn't even certain about that herself even though she'd witnessed his release. She turned on her heel and started toward the house. When she realized he wasn't moving, she looked over her shoulder and asked, "Are you coming?"

He gave her a nod and followed. Inside the kitchen, she noted his sudden discomfort. He stood stock still in the doorway. It seemed as if this new world closed in around him. Confusion filled his expression while he took in his surroundings. She touched his arm and smiled at him.

"Let me help you. I'm sure things are very different from your time." She pulled out a chair at the table and motioned for him to sit. He hesitated then removed his Claymore, hung it on the chair and sat.

Caledonia lifted the lid on the pot of stew Momma left for her to eat for dinner. She spoke as she worked. "This is a stove. I'm not sure how food was prepared during your time, but today we use this."

She pointed out the features of the stove, how it worked and the different knobs. She turned a knob and the gas-eye lit with a click. Struan watched without question but she noted his eyebrow arched when the flame appeared under the pot.

She took two glasses and two bowls from the cabinet. She filled the glasses with ice and water, explaining the refrigerator and the tap as she moved. Each time she looked at him, he appeared to be an attentive student absorbing everything like a dried sponge soaking up a large water spill. When he pointed to the ceiling, she followed his finger. His mumbled one-word question had her swallowing a laugh. In no way would she insult him. He needed to learn if he were to survive in this new age.

"Magic?"

Caledonia shook her head as she moved to the switch on the wall. "No, it's a ceiling lamp and it's powered by electricity. See?" She flicked the switch down, cutting the light and filling the room with total darkness, minus the glow from the flame under the pot on the stove. Instantly, she flicked it up and light flooded the room, making him blink. She returned to the stove, stirred the stew then filled the bowls.

"Here, Momma makes the best stew." She handed him a spoon then paused, not sure if they had utensils back then. He must've seen her hesitation as he spoke.

"We had spoons, bowls, pots. None o' this magic you call e-lec-tri-city." He stumbled over the word but got it out. "Our stove used wood for a fire. No running water as you have but we survived. Castle MacKinnon was the finest of its time." Pride filled his words. His chest puffed and his face beamed. "After we eat, I wish to go home."

Caledonia touched his hand. "Aye, after we eat."

Throughout the meal, she answered his questions. It impressed her that he listened, digested what she told him then chose his questions wisely. It was as if he strategically planned what he asked before doing so. His hunger for knowledge nearly matched his hunger for food. She filled his bowl four times before he claimed he'd had enough. She placed the bowls in the sink just as the back door opened and in walked her parents.

Struan sprang to his feet and drew his sword. Caledonia moved quickly to his side and gently touched his arm. "Struan, these are my parents, Aileen and Fin Kavanagh."

It eased the tightness in her chest to see his stance relax. *Whew, that was close.* Somehow she might need to relieve him of that sword before he accidentally skewered someone.

Caledonia's Poppa stepped around his wife the moment the sword had been drawn. His face heated red with anger. His fists raised, taking a fighter's stance facing off with Struan. "Who the hell do you think you are? This is my house and no one shall hurt my girls."

"The young man is Struan MacKinnon, dear. He just woke from a two-hundred-year nap," Momma stated as if it were a world-known fact. She hugged her husband from behind, laid her chin upon his shoulder and stretched to kiss his cheek. "He is a guest in our home. Now the two of you lower your weapons and make nice, while I fix us some tea."

"Are you daft, woman?" Fin sputtered as he continued to size up Struan. He bobbed and weaved, making ready to fight. "No one points a sword at me 'n my own house."

Struan sheathed his sword and offered his hand as he spoke. His head bowed but Caledonia doubted he took his eyes off Poppa. "My apologies, sir. Everything is new to me. Your entrance startled me. Please accept my hand in forgiveness. I had no right to draw my sword in your home."

"Take his hand, Fin," Momma encouraged as she set the kettle on to boil. "Or you may be sleeping on top o' the covers tonight instead o' under them." The look she leveled on Poppa made Caledonia smile inwardly. It was no secret her parents shared a *healthy*, happy relationship. One she hoped to find someday.

"But," Fin muttered. His fists dropped to his sides the moment Momma's eyebrows raised and her arms crossed under her breasts.

"Thank you," Momma said then turned to Caledonia. "Has he eaten?"

"Aye, Milady. You make a fine stew," Struan proclaimed. He rubbed his belly as a sign of his enjoyment.

"Good, I'm glad you liked it." Momma nodded. "Why don't we each take a seat and get to know one another over tea?"

"I'm gonna need something stronger to understand this one," Poppa claimed as he walked to the cabinet beside the refrigerator where they kept the whiskey. He retrieved the bottle and two shot glasses. Without asking, he put an empty glass in front of Struan then took a seat at the table across from him. He filled their glasses but neither drank. They simply watched each other.

"Caledonia, why don't you explain the situation to your poppa?" Aileen poured four cups of tea, set one in front of each then took a seat beside Fin with hers in hand.

She took a breath and prayed Poppa listened. Sometimes he had a tendency to be difficult, especially when it came to spirits and such. Boy, did this fall under the *and such* category. When she finished with the tale, he sat back, looked Struan up and down.

"So what you're saying, is if'n I go out to the shed, the statue won't be there because he's sitting here."

"Aye." Caledonia felt small under his unwavering stare, but remained vigilant in her attempt to make him understand she spoke the truth.

He stood without a word and walked out the back door. Caledonia rose to follow but her momma clasped her wrist. "Let him see with his own eyes. It'll sink in better."

Aileen rose from her chair and took a container from the refrigerator. She opened it and Struan's eyes widened. "Help yourself to shortbread. Baked fresh this morning. It'll go great with your second cup o' tea." She turned to fetch the still-hot kettle and tea bags. By the time she poured, Fin returned.

He flopped into his seat, lifted his untouched shot and nodded at Struan. "If'n I hadn't seen it with my own eyes, I would never have believed it. Here's to your freedom." He downed his whiskey.

Struan lifted the glass of amber liquid, nodded at Fin then tossed his back as well. "Aye, a mighty fine whiskey, Kavanagh."

"You may call me Fin."

"Poppa, Struan wants to return to his home at Castle MacKinnon in Lochsbury. I'm going to search my laptop for directions and drive him home tonight."

Poppa made a face. "That's not possible tonight, lass. I loaned the van to the O'Reilly boys. They took it down to Glassboro. Won't be back until in the morning."

Great, neither of the O'Reillys believed in carrying a cell phone so she had no way to reach them. "Why didn't they take that antique Land Rover they drive?"

"Blew a head gasket. That's why they borrowed the van in the first place, to drive down and pick one up. Then they decided they'd stay over and try out the nightlife." Fin nodded at Struan. "Another shot, *m'caraid*? Seems you're going to be here for another night."

Though he nodded, his smile was thin and Caledonia sensed his displeasure.

"Take it this way, Struan," Caledonia said. "It'll give you a night to acclimate to your new era."

"I do not understand this O'Reillys van thing. What does it have to do with me? I travel tonight, on foot, alone. I know the way."

"It's not necessary for you to walk," Caledonia interjected. "If you wait until the van is returned, I'll drive you there and it will only take a matter of hours instead of days."

"What is this van?" His head shook adamantly. "Is it a fast horse? Even so, I have never heard of a horse that could make the trip from Loch Tay to Castle MacKinnon in less than two days of steady travel."

Caledonia stifled the giggle that threatened, cleared her throat then smiled. "It's faster than a horse. Tomorrow, I will show it to you and explain its uses more clearly. I promise. Where exactly is Lochsbury?"

His face lightened and pride filled his words as he spoke of his home. "Lochsbury lies in the heart of the Grampian Mountains. Castle MacKinnon is the jewel of its center and provides for all of the people loyal to Clan

MacKinnon. My *brathairs*, *piuthar* and I strive to make sure not one soul perishes under our guidance."

The way his chest puffed and his chin tilted made him even more handsome in Caledonia's eyes. He placed much pride and honor in family and that ranked top on her list of priorities in life. Unlike Kip. She mentally shook the self-absorbed jerk from her thoughts. Across from her sat a true man, one who understood the meaning of family.

Why hadn't she been born during his time? *Then you would've missed out on him now*, whispered through her head and she realized she would've lost him to a curse. Fate had a way of dealing cruel blows sometimes. His life. His family. All were taken from him. Until now. Now it was up to her to get him home safely. Then what? Would she see him again? Would it end there? God, she hoped not. She wouldn't dwell on that. If it were meant to be between them, then it would be. She sighed softly, setting her resolve to help right things in Struan's topsy-turvy world.

"I look forward to seeing your home," Caledonia stated. She poured four shots of whiskey, set the bottle down then lifted her glass. "Here's to a new beginning in a new world."

* * * * *

Struan walked to the end of the dock and sat. His head ached. So much to learn in this new era, his thoughts tangled together with information that crowded his brain. New things flashed behind his eyes. Lights without flame, cooking with magic fire, so many devices he needed to learn to operate if he wanted to fit in. His hand dropped to the hilt of his Claymore at the memory of Caledonia suggesting he not carry it.

A man without a weapon, the thought was inconceivable. How did one protect his family and himself if attacked? His brows bunched. He pinched the bridge of his nose, trying to stave the onslaught of confusion from beating its way through his head. The throb increased. He breathed in deep and tried to relax. Eyes closed, he focused on his surroundings.

Peaceful sounds from his surroundings were a welcome harmony after years of silence. A breeze rustled the leaves of the tree to his left. Crickets chirped a lovely tune, which made him smile as he soaked it all in. He opened his eyes in time to see that roughly ten feet in front of him a monstrous fish breached the surface of the moonlit loch. If only he were prepared to fish. He sighed as he watched it disappear. He removed his boots, laid his *sgian dubh*, knife, at his side and lowered his feet into the soothing coolness of the loch.

The water called to him. It was his weakness. Where others shied from a swim, he thrived in it. Struan shucked off his Claymore and shirt then stood and dropped his kilt. A night swim would refresh his mind. A swim always did. Unsure of the depth, he stepped off the end instead of diving headfirst as his heart longed to do. It came to the top of his shoulders.

He swam toward the middle. Cutting the surface in solid strokes loosened his stiff muscles. Lack of use was the reason behind his body's tender state. He refused to let his mind dwell on the curse and that bastard MacGillivray. He was in the water, relaxing, letting it wash over him, taking away the sordid past events. Struan filled his lungs to capacity and dove. Though it was dark, he loved the sensation of the underworld enveloping him in its glorious folds. Being beneath the water's surface gave him peace.

Memories from the past controlled his direction. He knew this loch well. Many times he'd swam above and below as far as his strength and air would carry him. Though he could not see, images from his treasure chest of memories floated behind his eyes. Plants, rocks and fish appeared as if he were seeing them at that very moment. The sensation of fish swimming around him made him pause. Was it real or simply a figment of his imagination? Nothing brushed against him so he chose the latter. Imagination.

When he breached the surface for air, he swiped his hair from his eyes and floated on his back. Utter peacefulness whispered through his core. Water spurned his soul to life. It always had and this time was no different. It helped soothe his inner worries and untangled the knot of overwhelming information inside his head.

Had it truly been over two hundred years? Struan sorted through his thoughts. The loch appeared to have changed little, but the houses, people and things were definitely not the same. The Kavanaghs were good people. They'd sat for hours, talking and teaching him things they thought he needed to know. The beautiful Caledonia took the forefront of his thoughts. She stood at the sink doing dishes when he left the kitchen. He claimed he needed air and a moment to think. Her understanding touched him. Yet, she made him promise not to attempt to walk home.

A smile crossed his lips. Her concern warmed his insides and brought a renewed vigor to his shaft. Caledonia was a woman any man would be proud to have at his side. Struan did a strong backstroke, guiding his course toward the dock. So many things had changed, even the people and especially the women. If things were different, he'd take his time savoring every inch of Caledonia. His mouth watered for want of a taste of her lips, her breasts and the heaven between her thighs, which he imagined would be a delightful blend of woman and roses.

Struan paused mid-stroke. Never had he been so bold with his thoughts of a woman he did not know. With Mary, he'd not so much as kissed her in all their years as friends. Why? Because she was betrothed to another and it went against society's rules. Still, he had loved her. But it was a love that could never be and just as he had accepted it as unchangeable then, he accepted it now. He closed his eyes and issued a silent prayer for her soul's final entrance into the Garden of Angels and a peaceful rest.

Through the fog of his thoughts, Caledonia stepped forward to reign supreme in her beautiful image behind his closed lids. He imagined perfect womanly curves, which beckoned to his natural instinct to mate. Something about her ignited his lust and triggered an undeniable need. Though he tried to control it, his shaft reacted. *Wonderful.* He snorted, thankful it was still dark though the time for the sun's rise neared. If not, all would see his rendition of a ship with its staff held high for the raising of the flag.

With little splash, he rolled over and dove, hoping the colder water would ease his condition. As he swam, he plotted his course. He needed to return to Castle MacKinnon and his family. They needed him. Two others were found. He was free. Four remained lost. He lingered on those still lost. Padon. Aiden. And the twins, Donnell and Dour. Need of a different sort barreled through him, forcing him to surface. Home called to his heart and gnawed at his soul.

Deep in his gut he knew he wasn't ready to return home even though his heart weighed heavy with the desire to seek refuge in his family's arms. Something bound him here to Loch Tay. A haunting ache tugged at his soul. The sense that a small part of his spirit still laid upon the bottom gripped his thoughts, refusing to allow him peace. Maybe once he was away from this place the annoying sensation would cease and he would be free to live his life as a man again.

Struan broke the water and wasted no time closing the distance to the dock. Though the water invigorated and renewed his strength, loyalty beckoned him home to Castle MacKinnon. Without much effort, he lifted onto the dock and stood, coming upright to face Caledonia. How long had she been there?

The nervous dart of her tongue across her bottom lip issued an invitation he hungered to accept but refused. She stood, hands at her sides, silent, gaze leveled on his. Those beautiful, full breasts pressed taut against her shirt, tempting his tongue to lave them with affection. Lust battled loyalty. Desire hardened his shaft and tightened his bawl sac. Now was not the time for personal pleasure. These sudden urges and rampant desires had to be some sort of aftereffect of the curse, Struan decided. But he would resist. Caledonia deserved his respect, not his shaft.

Though nudity bothered him none, he whisked his kilt into position low upon his hips then tugged on his tunic. If he didn't, he knew he'd act upon his lust. Caledonia deserved more than to be treated like one of the bawdy wanton slappers he'd visited for mindless pleasure in his time. She deserved to be treated like a lady and from this moment forth, he intended to treat her as such, no matter how much it hurt his bawls. Her strained voice broke through his aggravated train of thought and he sensed she struggled just as he with the ravages of unrequited desire.

Seeing him cut the water like a fish took her breath away. Did he love the water as much as she? The moon brightened his muscular backside with each stroke and when he dove out of sight, her heart dropped. Endless seconds passed before he surfaced and Caledonia released the breath she inadvertently held until she caught sight of him again. It appeared as if he enjoyed it. Did he do it as a form of a bath or out of the simple joy of the swim? She ached to know.

Caledonia struggled with the sudden desire to join him. The water was her second home, a natural place for her to relax. Should she strip and dive in? Watching him float had her torn with indecision. He had asked for a moment alone, to think and gather his thoughts. So much challenged him, his past, his present and the unknown of his future. True, they'd bombarded him with information to the point she'd sensed he'd overloaded and became inwardly distraught.

God, if she were in his shoes. She wrung her hands, fighting the desire to go to him and share in the joy and freedom the loch provided the soul. Though it excited her to see he sought solace from the loch such as she, she remained vigilant in her oath to help him find his way. She tried to look away from the graceful litheness of his movements but couldn't. He belonged as if the water and he were one.

A heavy, contented sigh escaped and she knew a little piece of her heart had been lost to the hot, sexy laird swimming the loch. Caledonia couldn't move when he reached the dock. With a fluidity and style all his own, Struan rose from the water and lifted to his feet in front of her as if it were as natural as breathing. She swallowed against the sudden need to kiss his lips and plow her hands through his wet hair. The fact he had a hard-on didn't help her resistance strategy any.

Focus, she ordered. Focus on helping him understand his new life. Thankfully, he dressed, helping her if only a smidgeon of an ounce to maintain her dignity and not pounce on him and fuck him right there. The one thing in her favor was the sound of fishermen around the loch making ready to set sail for the day, echoing on the early-morning breeze. Knowing the sun's rays would soon break helped keep her clothes on and her raging libido controlled, if only for the moment. She definitely didn't want the whole fishing community to see her butt naked, frolicking with a man on the dock. In a small village such as this, it would be the talk of the century.

"You like to swim?"

Caledonia waited for his response to her question. Did he or didn't he?

"Aye," he finally replied, tugged on one of his boots and slipped something she didn't quite see well into it. A knife perhaps? "I love a good swim every now and again. It refreshes the soul."

Refreshes the soul. Had she heard him right? Yeah, she did. Caledonia smiled. A man who liked water, unlike Kip who only used it for the hidden treasures he sold to line his pockets.

"I noticed you dove under. How far can you go on a single breath?" She tried not to let her excitement show in her voice, but she knew from his partial smile he picked up on it.

"Not as far as I would like," he replied as he looked out over the loch and slung his Claymore in place. "The water calls to me. I have always enjoyed the pleasure it provides my soul."

"Would you like to reach the bottom?"

His brows bunched. "Not possible. It is endless."

"Nay." Caledonia shook her head as she smiled. "It is not. That is where I found you." She pointed in the direction of his former grave. "With the proper diving equipment and training, reaching the bottom of the loch is possible."

His face grew solemn and his eyes held a lost appeal. "You found me on the bottom o' Loch Tay?"

Caledonia stood beside him and laid her hand upon his shoulder in comfort. "Aye. It wasn't how Mary meant for you to be hidden. I'm guessing she knew of your love for the water. They built a special boat in the shape of a floating crannog, chained it in the center of the standing remains of four crannogs and set you to float in the safety of this sanctuary. No one could reach you before being spotted by the castle's watchtower guards. In Mary's words, it was the perfect hiding place."

She took a moment and let that sink in before she began again. "The summer before Mary's death, a storm of tremendous force ripped through the area. It destroyed much of the surrounding village and caused the weakened structures of the crannogs to sink. The weight of the crannogs dragged your boat to the bottom. There was no saving you."

Cupping his chin, she turned his gaze to meet hers. An unreadable look lingered in his eyes. Was he angry? Saddened? She couldn't be sure. "Mary never meant for you to sink to the bottom of Loch Tay. She simply hid you where she thought you'd most want to be. Near the water."

"Aye," he stated in a heavy, disheartened tone. "Nature granted my wish though my eyes were cursed and could not enjoy the beauty o' what lay deep beneath its surface."

He stepped away from her and returned his stare to the water. Caledonia refused to let it go. Her heart brimmed with the need to help him, to make him understand that she could and would make that wish come true for him.

"If you're willing to learn, I'm willing to teach you. I've been to the bottom of Loch Tay."

"How has a wee lass such as yourself been to the bottom?"

She ignored the scoff in his tone. Her eyebrow arched and she smiled. "If I didn't reach the bottom, how did you return to the surface?"

His mouth opened then shut and she knew he had no clue. "Come with me," Caledonia said as she turned and headed for the shed. "I'll show you the magic of my world and if you're a good lad..." She shot him a naughty look across her shoulder. "I'll teach you how to dive and you too can reach the bottom."

She continued walking and hoped he followed. By the time she reached the doors, he was right behind her. They entered the dive shop just as the first rays of morning sun cracked the sky.

A tingle sizzled down her spine. The hairs on her arms and the back of her neck stood on end. A sudden burst of heat shot across her back and she was afraid to look. Oh God, she'd forgotten the last words of the anti-curse until that very moment.

Stone by day. Man by night.

Her legs knotted, not letting her turn until she forced them to work. Slowly she moved, hoping with every millisecond that passed, she was wrong. Her heart sank at the sight and her lungs refused to function.

Struan stood at full height, legs slightly apart, hair hung loosely down his back and across his shoulder and his arms at his sides. Not the same position in which they found him. How was she going to explain this when the O'Reillys returned? And most of all, how was she going to get him home in this condition?

Chapter Six

One moment he followed the beautiful and voluptuous Caledonia, and the next he'd been recaptured. Darkness surrounded him within a split second of fiery pain and a molten-hot series of spears shot through his body. *Och*, had he been cursed again? No witch's words reached his ears prior to being taken prisoner. Simply a change in the time. Night gave way to day. He saw and heard nothing that garnered his imprisonment. It must have been some form of a sneak attack, from behind or hidden within the shadows of the shed.

Not certain where he was or how this happened, Struan attempted to move. No part of his being followed his internal commands. *Arm lift, draw thy sword*, he shouted mentally. Nothing happened. *Eyes open*, he demanded. They also failed to respond. Though he tried, his lungs required no breath. Did his heart beat? Aye, he felt certain it did, even if he had no true means to test it.

Inwardly, he struggled to free himself until his mind became exhausted. Madness threatened to rule his thoughts. Trapped with no means of escape. How had this happened? Why? Had Mary not said two of his *brathairs* were free? Then why not him? What had he done to fall twice to this curse?

Struan drew upon his faith to soothe his angst. Love for family, pride, honor and a renewed vigor for life combined within his soul, washing over him with a sense of inner peace. There had to be a way to escape. It happened once. It would happen again. Of this he felt certain. Caledonia would see to it.

Caledonia. Though guilt laced his thoughts, her image filled his mind's eye. Long, dark tresses flowed freely across her shoulders to her waist. Naked, she stood before him. A vision of pure woman ripened to perfection and ready to be plucked by the right man. Was he that man? If his face would obey, a smile would have stretched his lips.

Between strands of silken hair, nipples peeked, beckoning his mouth to sample.

He knew he shouldn't think like this, but his mind refused to listen. *Och*, how he wished he could move. If he could move, then maybe he could redirect his line of thought to something less stimulating. Try as he might, no other images prevailed.

The scent of rose haunted his memory, bringing Caledonia even more to life in his head. He hungered to taste her lips, her skin, those pert nipples. Caledonia's breasts filled his hands, heavy yet soft and pliable with plump, teaseable nipples. He knew his mouth would water if it could. Damn, he hated being trapped.

Pressure threatened to crush him. Darkness kept him encapsulated in its dismal folds. No escape. No way out. Struan dug deep for the strength to curtail this sudden rush of panic. Refusing to let the walls close in on him, he tried to redirect his focus on something to calm his nerves. Caledonia's image reappeared. That last sight of her walking in front of him, the gentle sway of those full hips, ignited his lust as if it were a match and he the wick.

Och, it killed him that he could not react to the images inside his head or stop them.

An idea shot from the back of his brain like a fast-flying arrow. Pleasing her—if only in his head—would keep him occupied to distraction until the path to escape made itself clear. *A winning strategy worked best when not over-planned. Relax, watch and listen, all shall reveal itself in time.* His *brathair* Gaven's words resurfaced to the forefront and gave him the added boost in confidence needed. How many times had his *brathair's* straightforward, clear-cut wisdom guided him in the right direction? Too many to count. Struan inwardly laughed.

Hopefully madness would not consume him before Caledonia found a way to release him again. Struan willed peace to settle in his soul and let Caledonia's beautiful image soothe his angst. He focused on her face and issued a mental prayer.

Save me, Caledonia. Set me free.

* * * * *

By noon, they had a plan in place. Fin and Aileen Kavanagh took the trawler and headed north to Balloch Castle where they used a small forklift to move heavy materials for the hotel. Fin called in a favor in order to borrow it. Caledonia promised she'd get some rest while they were gone. She'd been up all night with Struan and well into the morning pacing, waiting on the O'Reillys to return.

God, what was keeping them? Hangovers. She'd bet the boat on it. She waved to Momma and Poppa as they pulled away from the dock. Exhaustion threatened to make her collapse where she stood. Something made her double-check the locks on the shed. Struan was safe. No one would harm him here.

Tired legs carried her to the house. She didn't have the strength to tackle the hike upstairs to her bedroom. Instead, she curled up on the soft, comfy sofa in the family room. Tabby's kittens followed her and settled on the rug beside the couch. Except for one—the only male in the litter. The gray with the jet-black stripe down his back refused to leave her alone until she lifted him onto the couch with her.

"I think I'll call you Streak," Caledonia whispered against his fur as the kitten snuggled close. Sunlight warmed her face and lulled her into a tranquil state of rest. Nothing could have roused her from the dream of diving the loch with a hot Scottish laird.

Eyelids fluttered with images of Struan donning a neoprene body suit for diving. He smiled at her as they did the final check before tumbling off the rail of the *Marcail Struana* and into Loch Tay. Joy and wonderment rippled off him in waves as they descended. It filled her heart to share this with him, the love of the dive, the exploration of the unknown. Watching him dive as if it were second nature sent a thrill to her core. Together, they blossomed in the peacefulness of the underworld.

Thigh brushed thigh. Arm touched arm. The form-fitting drysuit molded to his massive size, making him even sexier in her eyes. The neoprene stretched taut across his broad chest, abs, biceps and thighs. His bottom looked inviting and it took a great act of resistance not to playfully slap that solid mound of muscle. At her side, he moved in sync with her underwater rhythm, touching her gently. Tiny tremors skittered across her flesh beneath her drysuit.

Like magic, their suits disappeared and it didn't matter they had no breathing apparatus. It was a dream. Caledonia didn't panic. She let the vision override common sense and snuggled into the depths of a perfect moment suspended in the confines of her mind. He reached for her. Mouth upon mouth, they kissed. Tongues interlocked in a war of passion. Deeper they descended until two bodies connected as one lay on a bed of underwater foliage at the bottom of the loch.

The outside world disappeared. There was nothing but her, Struan and the phenomenal gifts of Loch Tay swimming around them.

Hours later she woke to the ring of the telephone. Caledonia sat upright. The clock claimed it was two. Had she truly dozed off for several hours? Momma, Poppa, had they returned? *Ring. Ring.* She jumped to answer the phone. In a voice groggy from sleep, she answered, "Hello."

"Hey, Caledonia," Percy stated cheerfully. "How's everything on your end?"

"Fine," she managed to reply as she tried to brush off the last remnants of her nap. "What time are you and Able bringing the van back?"

"Not until tomorrow," he said. "The auto shop had to order the part and it won't be in until the morning. That's why I'm calling. Is your poppa around? I need to make sure it's all right to just hang here until then and drive back as soon as we have the part."

Her brain kicked into gear with an idea that made her heart flutter. This gave her another day with Struan. But would he be happy when he woke and found himself still at Loch Tay and not home? Caledonia chewed her lower lip. Struan did say he wanted to learn to dive. Maybe this little setback wasn't really a setback at all. The lingering effects of euphoria from her dream drove her to her next decision. She planned to make at least one of his wishes come true before he returned to Castle MacKinnon. A grin split her lips.

"Percy, you guys keep the van," she said. "Just let me know where you're staying in case of an emergency. You know, this wouldn't be a problem if you agreed to carry a cell phone."

Percy's laugh made her smile. She knew his reply even before he said it. "Cell phones are for yuppies. Do you remember Big Mike from the salvage crew?"

"Yeah," she replied. Who could forget a man who stood around six foot four and weighed in at about three hundred pounds? Though he was large, he handled the equipment with the style and grace of a ballerina. There wasn't anything he couldn't fix.

"We ran into him last night and you're never going to believe what he told us. Hang on, Caledonia," Percy said. She heard him answering Able in the background but couldn't understand the conversation. He must've covered the receiver with his hand to muffle the sound. "Sorry about that. I've got to go. Remind me when I get back to fill you in on the details. You're going to love it. We're staying at Big Mike's. Take down this number and we'll see you tomorrow."

She wrote down the number he recited.

"You guys don't still happen to have that diving suit of his, do you? You know, the one we found in the bottom of that crate of stuff Kip shipped to me right after the divorce?" She crossed her fingers and prayed they hadn't been responsible enough to return it or throw it out. When he answered, she smiled.

"Yeah, it's still in the bottom of that crate in the back corner of the shed," Percy replied. "If I knew we were going to run into him, I would've brought it with us and returned it. I've really got to go. Able and Mike are waiting."

She couldn't tell him she was happy he hadn't done as she asked so many months ago. It was probably the only suit in existence that would possibly fit Struan. Caledonia looked to the heavens and issued a silent word of thanks the suit was still in the shed. She leaned against the wall beside the kitchen phone after hanging up. One more day with Struan. She couldn't help but smile. Then it hit her. He wouldn't wake until dark. She rarely dove after dark. This was going to be a whole new experience for her.

She shoved off the wall and nearly tripped over Streak. His pissed meow let Caledonia know he didn't like being ignored. She scooped him up and headed out the back door. Several hours separated her from Struan and she wanted to have everything in place and ready to go when he woke.

* * * * *

It was late afternoon when she finally opened the shed doors. "Ah," he sighed. There it sat. Sun glistened off the majestic statue. He focused the telephoto lens. Odd, it seemed positioned differently than he remembered. Maybe it was because they had it turned facing inside the shed instead of out like it was yesterday. He shrugged. It didn't matter. All he needed was evidence a valuable find such as this existed.

Click. Click. Click. He took multiple shots, hoping for at least one good one to post online. His hand faltered and his mouth dropped open. What the hell was she doing? He zoomed in on Caledonia. She held several different diving masks and kept switching from one to the other as if she were sizing him up for a perfect fit. After a couple of tries, she seemed to have found the right one because she placed it on the statue's head and left it there.

Kip's brows bunched. Had she lost her mind? She disappeared into the far corner of the shed out of view. No matter how hard he tried, he couldn't see what she was doing from his position hidden in the trees directly across Loch Tay. He didn't have to wait long to find out.

He couldn't believe what he saw through the camera. Caledonia stretched an oversized diving suit between her hands and held it up to the statue's back. Was she seeing if it would fit? Oh lord, had she been drinking? That had to be the reason behind her playing dress-up with the statue. At least that was the one he was going with for lack of a better idea. The longer he watched, the more her actions befuddled him.

It appeared as if she prepared for a dive. She checked and rechecked equipment. He even thought it looked like she was talking to the statue. He knew for a fact no one else was in the dive shed with her. The OReillys left the day before with the van and her parents took the boat out earlier and had not returned as of yet. So he was reasonably sure she *was* talking to the statue.

"Oh, Caledonia," he whispered. "Why can't you see you need me? Without me, you've gone mental."

* * * * *

When her parents returned, she explained the new plan. Because the O'Reillys got tied up in Glassboro, she decided to teach Struan to dive, which turned out to be a good thing. Poppa was unable to borrow the forklift. When they arrived so did an unexpected delivery of heavy materials needed for renovations being done at the hotel.

"Looks like this was meant to be," Momma said as she patted Caledonia's shoulder. "I'll make dinner and hold it for when you're done."

"Thank you." Caledonia kissed her momma's cheek.

Poppa watched Momma until she was inside the back door. He spun to face Caledonia. "I've got some bad news. Kip is staying at the hotel. He hasn't left."

"What?" Caledonia couldn't believe Kip hung around. "Are you sure?"

"Aye," Poppa said, nodding his head. "Fergus saw him earlier, leaving the hotel."

"Any luck he checked out?" Caledonia asked though she had a sinking feeling he hadn't.

"Nope, and you can bet he's up to something," Poppa replied in a tone filled with distrust. "I feel it all the way to my bones."

Caledonia didn't say a word. She felt it too. Mistrust for the man she used to call husband boiled in her gut. She knew him too well. He wasn't one to hang around and enjoy the sights. So why was he still here? Was he watching her or was he after something else? In a slow-motion sweep, she scanned the landscape for possible signs of Kip. Her spine tightened at the thought he might try and steal from her again.

A quick glint of light caught her eye from the wooded area across the lake. And she instantly knew Poppa had seen it as well.

"Did you see that?" he asked, pointing in its direction.

It disappeared before she got a good bead on its actual location. Was someone hiding in there? No. She shook her head. Even Kip knew better than to do something as stupid as spy on her. Or was he? Caledonia took a deep breath and tried to reason with this sudden onset of jitters and her poppa. "The light was probably the sun bouncing off a hiker's piece of gear," she said, trying to sound convincing.

She heard Poppa shuffling through a cabinet in the shed. Seconds later he held the replica pirate's eyeglass she'd given him for his birthday. He placed it to his eye and turned the end, focusing the lens. As if searching for an enemy ship on the high seas, he scanned the opposite bank.

"Somebody's hightailing it out of there," he stated. "But I can't get a good look at him. The trees are in the way."

Caledonia snorted. Without seeing the person, she had a gut feeling it was Kip. With the sun sitting low on the horizon, she decided it was best to close the shed doors. No need for him—or anyone else for that matter—to see Struan's release. It would be hard to explain. Poppa followed suit and grabbed the other door and helped her close them tight. Together they waited.

It seemed like an eternity before the sun's last rays left the sky. The ground around them vibrated. The air sizzled with sudden heat. Every hair on the back of her neck and arms lifted as energy rippled through her core. Struan was waking. The stone split and light shot from it, filling the room for a second with blinding brightness. She heard his first gasp for air before her eyes adjusted and she saw him. Looking disoriented but alive, Struan stood in the exact spot where the curse took him the night before, just inside the doorway.

"Caledonia." His first word spoken was her name and it thrilled her to hear him say it. She stepped forward and cupped his face with her palm.

"It's good to see you awake again, Struan." She smiled as she met his questioning gaze.

"What happened?" he asked, confusion haunting his features.

"The curse isn't entirely broken," Caledonia said. "Unfortunately, you turn back into stone when the sun rises and you are released at nightfall."

His mouth opened as if to speak but closed just as quickly. Mixed emotions crossed his face—confusion, sadness then anger. All of which she understood. If she were in his shoes, she didn't doubt she'd suffer from every conflicting sensation the body produced.

"Struan," Caledonia spoke softly without releasing his wary gaze. "Would you like to learn to dive? To reach the bottom of Loch Tay?"

She liked the fact he didn't hesitate in his answer. "Aye."

"Then you're in luck," she stated cheerfully, hoping to uplift his mood before giving him more bad news. "I'd like to give you your first diving lesson tonight. Are you interested?"

"Though the temptation you present me is great, I would like to return to Castle MacKinnon."

"Unfortunately," Fin stated as he placed a hand on Struan's shoulder. "That's not a possibility tonight. We are still without the van until the morning. So *m'cariad*, you might as well relax and enjoy an evening in the loch."

Though she sensed he struggled inwardly over his predicament, he nodded. "Aye."

"Then let's get you suited up and taught how to use the equipment." She may not have the answer to end the curse, but at least she could share the love of the water with him and hopefully give him an ounce of joy by doing so.

Chapter Seven

He took the items she handed him and held them at arm's length as he examined them. The suit was made of something soft and it stretched when he pulled it. He held the mask to his face and looked through it. When Caledonia helped fit it properly on his face, he couldn't help but blink repeatedly as a fog coated the inside.

He snatched it off his head, exclaiming, "How does this help one see? It hinders my breathing and created a fog through which I could not see. "

"I'll show you," Caledonia explained patiently. She grabbed another mask and positioned it on her face with the strap across her head. She sounded funny when she spoke. "You have to breathe through your mouth and not your nose. That way it doesn't fog up so you can see. Also, I'll show you another trick that will help keep that from happening once we're in the water. Now, let's get that suit on you."

She removed the mask, turned and stripped in front of him. His lips parted slightly and his breath hitched in his throat at the sight of her shirt lift. His eyebrow arched and puzzlement twisted his perception at the color of her skin. Green? Curiosity guided his hand. Without asking, he touched her tummy. She jumped, snatched the shirt off over her head and stared wide-eyed at him.

"I apologize," he said sincerely, dropping his hand to his side. "I have never seen green skin."

Caledonia looked down and he noted her expression light with humor. Her lips trembled slightly and he knew she fought the urge to laugh. After a moment, she returned her gaze to his and explained, pulling the fabric from her and releasing it with a snap.

"This is a bathing suit. It fits tight. Most people wear them when they swim." This time she didn't even attempt to halt the smile, which made him smile as well. "Not everyone skinny dips like you do."

"Explain this skinny dip," he requested even though he had an inkling it meant swimming naked.

He liked the way a light-red hue brushed her cheeks as she licked her lips then found the courage to answer. "Skinny dipping is what you did last night."

Struan couldn't help teasing her. Leaning in close to her ear, the whispered response left his lips before he thought better of it. "Ah, you mean naked. That is how I prefer to be. Swimming and in bed."

Instantly, the light hue turned a brighter shade and he didn't even attempt to hide his amusement. Sliding a finger beneath her chin, he tilted her face, which was a mistake. If he leaned even the slightest bit, their lips were within kissing distance. Desire rippled through his core at the memory of her sweet taste. He also remembered the accurate aim of her knee. Before he stepped back, he said, "Caledonia, you are even more beautiful when you blush. You remind me o' my sister. Easily teased, yet filled with the inner strength befitting o' any man."

"If you want to learn to dive, then you better think twice about teasing the teacher," she quipped.

She stepped away from him and grabbed a suit similar to the one he held but much smaller. The fire that burned within her delighted him. A woman with a feisty spirit. He liked that. Struan once again held the suit in front of him and stretched it.

Looking over at Caledonia, his jaw dropped and he concentrated hard to prevent his tongue from lolling out his mouth at the sight of her trews hitting the floor. Though her bottom was wrapped in the green clothing she called a bathing suit, he couldn't help but notice her perfect womanly shape. The image of his hands on her arse, kneading it as he held her close speared his brain and knotted his bawls. Quickly, he looked at the suit in his hands. Need flashed to life within him. Hunger for a woman's touch watered his soul and made his shaft twitch.

Och, Caledonia was all woman. He closed his eyes and dug for a measure of control over the rampant rush of pure lust. Deep in concentration, he missed what she said. He cleared his throat then turned his gaze to her, making sure he aimed his eyes at her face.

"Excuse me. I was not listening."

"Well, at least you admit it, most men don't," she stated and he noted the concern in her tone as well as in her gaze. "It's really important you pay attention or would you rather not dive tonight?"

He shook his head as he found his voice. "Nay, Caledonia. I wish to learn. Please teach me how you reached the bottom o' Loch Tay and saved me from my watery grave. I promise to be the perfect student."

Caledonia was impressed with his ability to learn quickly. He listened, repeated what she told him then practiced what she'd taught. Over and over, she preached the basic safety steps, the use of the equipment and how it worked before she finally was able to get him suited up. She'd shown him how to put the suit on by stepping into hers. When he began to strip, she spun around, giving him her back. With Poppa's help, he was able to get the suit on, properly.

He wore a borrowed bathing suit beneath the neoprene diving suit. The way the diving suit fit had her insides twisted with the desire to peel it off him and taste him inch by succulent inch. Caledonia swallowed hard and mentally reissued the silent warning she kept giving herself. *He is your diving student. Teach him. Don't think about how hot he looks.* But it was damn hard not to drink him in from head to toe every time she looked his way. Neoprene never looked so fine. Eyes squeezed shut. She tried desperately to force the image from her mind, but failed miserably. It didn't help when she opened them and he stood beside her.

"Okay, walk down the dock and we'll take it from there," she said offhandedly. It took a great amount of mental strain to stall the sexual images flipping inside her brain, but she managed to force her focus on diving. At least for the moment. She huffed, trying not to stare at his arse as she followed him. "Let's start your first underwater lesson. We'll go off the end of the dock and stay close to shore until you get the hang of everything."

He held his hand to her and though she hesitated, she took it. He lifted it to his lips and placed a tender kiss to her knuckles. "Thank you," he whispered right before he released her.

The touch tore through her, sending instant need to her core. Damn, this wasn't good. Caledonia turned to face Poppa. He followed them, pushing a small cart carrying their supplies. Poppa handed them the masks, flippers, and scuba tanks. Caledonia placed her mask so it sat on her forehead. Struan did the same, mimicking her every move. He put on his flippers like she showed him. Like a pair of ducks, they waddled to the end of the dock with the scuba tanks on their backs.

Caledonia lowered her mask, looked at Struan and asked, "Are you ready to give this a try?"

"Aye," he replied, tugging his mask on properly.

She nodded at him then stepped off the end of the dock. Though the water was cold, it did nothing to cool the desire for her student. Struan entered right behind her. Caledonia tucked her regulator in her mouth and guided him through his first lesson on actually using the diving paraphernalia underwater. Repeatedly, she reinforced the emergency scenarios they'd practiced making sure he understood. When she felt confident he had them down pat, she led him on his first official dive.

Together they explored using underwater flashlights. She somehow managed to keep him to within fifty feet of the shoreline even though he urged her to go deeper. He wasn't ready. In her experience he needed a few dives under his belt in less than thirty feet before she'd venture farther.

Each time they returned to the dock to rest, his excitement warmed her soul. It had been all she could do to make him take breaks long enough to eat, relax, and go over the equipment again before they returned to the water. She gave him a map of the loch and together they marked the areas he explored that night. They repeated this scenario several times.

Struan's agility and quick-learning ability astounded her. He took to the water like a natural, which made her heart swell. The man was perfect. Remnants of her dream filtered through her thoughts each time he brushed against her. A thigh-to-thigh touch nearly undid her focus on teaching. And when he swam in front of her, the sight of slick neoprene pulled taut across his buns almost made her choke on her regulator.

Yeah, the man was perfect. She squeezed her eyes shut against the flood of sexual images caused by Struan in a tight diving suit. This was killing her, but she could do it. Redirecting her energy to the task at hand, she was determined he enjoy his first venture underwater with her as his teacher. Hopefully, he'd want to do it again. She made the wish as she opened her eyes.

Several feet ahead, Struan plundered the underworld with the excitement of a kid at Christmas. Seeing his flashlight beam dart from one thing to the next made her smile inwardly. *Idiot!* she scolded. *He's having fun and you're being a dirty-minded soul.* But boy, she bet sex with Struan while diving would probably blow her mind. Caledonia's watch flashed abruptly, interrupting her deviant thoughts and alerting her it was time to surface.

The sun would rise soon and there was no way she wanted him turning to stone while diving. It'd be a hell of a thing to have to explain to the O'Reillys as to why they were hauling the statue up from the bottom a second time. And worse, explaining how it got there.

She swam over to him and tapped him on the shoulder. With a hand gesture, she let him know they had to surface. Instant disappointment shone in his eyes. Caledonia lowered the light from his face. It hurt her heart to have to make him leave the water again but she had no choice. Time played against them. She led and he followed as they returned to the dock. Caledonia tossed her mask and fins onto the dock. She grabbed the ladder and lifted out of the water. When she slipped, a strong hand cupped her bottom and kept her from falling.

Moisture from something other than the loch formed between her thighs and she shivered. Never had she been this sexually excited by a simple touch of a hand to her arse. Caledonia swallowed against the knot in her throat and regained her balance. She quickly scooted onto the dock then turned to help Struan. He handed her his fins then lifted onto the dock without using the ladder. Pure strength rippled from him as he exited the loch with ease.

Excitement filled his voice as he spoke. "Caledonia, that was the most exquisite experience. Can we do it again?"

Her heart pounded and sank at the same time. It made her extremely happy to know he loved to dive and wanted to do it again. She also knew he wanted to return home as well. "We can. But not now, we're running out of night. And tomorrow the van should be back and I promised to take you home."

Silence fell between them and she noted a change in him. It appeared as if he struggled with a decision, but she kept quiet and didn't ask what was on his mind. He helped Caledonia with her scuba tank, then removed his and carried them both as they walked toward the shed. He returned the tanks to their proper place in the rack and hung a red tag on each that would let the others know which ones had been recently used. Caledonia couldn't help but smile at the fact he'd remembered her instructions right down to the minor detail of red tagging.

Struan straightened and turned to face her. His eyes seemed to sparkle and the joy in his tone couldn't be missed, letting her know he spoke from the heart. "Caledonia, you have given me a great adventure. One I shall never forget." He paused, looked around the room then returned a heated gaze directly on her.

Raw need battled her conscience in her desperate struggle to keep her hands at her sides and not peel the diving suit from his flesh and taste him from head to toe. Those eyes of his could melt butter. She was certain of it with the way he'd warmed her insides with just a hot, sexy look. When he closed the gap between them, she couldn't move. Every ounce of her wanted him to kiss her. He took her hand in his and kept his eyes leveled on hers.

"There is something I need to do before you return me to my home," he said. "And you are the only one who can help me with it. Are you willing to take me to the bottom o' Loch Tay? I want to see my watery grave before I return to Castle MacKinnon. I want to lay to rest my past and start my future without regrets." He lifted her hand and laid a tender kiss to her knuckles without releasing her gaze.

The look in his eyes portrayed desire mixed with a deeply haunted sadness, which tore at her heart. There was nothing she would deny him, not when he looked at her like a lost soul in need of guidance.

"Aye, Struan," she replied, swallowing the sudden excitement welling in her core. He wanted to stay and dive more with her. It wasn't about her, she reminded herself, it was about his need for closure. Inside her emotions tumbled in a mixed array of joy compounded by lust and confused by the noble side of her conscience to help.

She cleared her throat and managed to state, "I will help you. But it will take a series of dives and weeks of training to prepare you to reach that depth. It's not a simple task. Are you sure you want to do this? Don't you want to see your family?"

"My family has waited for my return for over two hundred years," he replied, cupping her cheek. He caressed her lower lip with his thumb and it was all she could do not to sample it between her teeth and suck the salt from his skin. "I do not think a few more days will matter."

His smile brightened his eyes yet the haunted sadness lingered in their depths. It was then she decided no matter what it took, she intended to help make that sadness disappear. Caledonia smiled.

"Okay, Struan. I'll help you reach the bottom."

Struan's reaction took her by surprise. He grabbed her around the waist and spun her around in his arms as he laughed loud and hearty. She couldn't help but laugh with him, even though being wrapped in those big, strong arms wreaked havoc on her. She wanted his hands on her, holding her, kneading her flesh and molding her breasts in his palms. God, this was truly going to be a test of her ability to refrain from sexually attacking her pupil.

As he slowed in his spinning of her, their gazes met. Silence weighed heavily between them. Caledonia couldn't help but hunger for his kiss and he didn't disappoint. Struan kissed her. Gently at first then their mutual desire controlled their actions, turning it into a passionate mouth on mouth, tongue tangled with tongue kiss of pure lust. Caledonia laced her fingers in his hair.

Struan cupped her breast with one hand, while his other hand caressed her back in a sensual massage along her spine. His hand lowered to her bottom, tugging her tighter against him. The taut neoprene diving suit outlined his solid cock pressed firmly against her lower abdomen. She wanted him and he wanted her. Caledonia broke from the kiss, placing tender kisses and nips to his lips, his jaw and his neck. She had to have him. Nothing would stop this, not now.

She worked her hand in-between them and pressed her palm to his distended member. She heard his muffled gasp against the top of her head as he nuzzled her hair. She liked the way he whispered her name as he released her breast and gathered her face in his hand. "Caledonia."

Their mouths connected again. The fire of desire flowed through her veins and she knew there was nothing that would ease the growing ache within her but to have Struan buried deep inside. She was lost in the arms of an ancient Scottish laird. Fate laid down a cruel card.

The first rays of morning light broke the sky. Heat sizzled in the air and Struan reacted instantly. He released her so quickly she stumbled backwards. His actions managed to place a gap between them a second before the curse snatched him into its folds. Frozen in stone, his statue portrayed a new position. Dressed in a diving suit, slightly bent at the waist, legs spread apart, arms outstretched and a look of strained surprise on his face.

Bewildered, Caledonia grappled for control over her reality. Fierce emotions zinged uncontrollably, while unrequited desire ripped through her core. Caledonia stood on trembling legs and stared. Thoughts tumbled inside her brain. Though she knew he'd fall to the curse at daybreak, it still disturbed her.

Studying his face, she interpreted the look as one of surprised fear. Was it fear that she might get caught in it if they touched when he returned to stone? Would she? Would she become stone if they touched as the curse resumed its vindictive hold upon his soul? The diving suit turned to stone. Did his kilt and other belongings change as well or did they have to be on him? She needed to know. Caledonia walked to the table and touched the neatly folded pile of his clothes.

Lifting his shirt, she fingered the material. His scent filled her nose. Pure masculinity mixed with fresh morning air. She gathered his shirt to her chest in an empty hug. His clothes held his smell, which soothed her tattered nerves. His sword she left on the table along with his boots, *sgian dubh*, and sporran. His shirt and kilt, she decided to take into the house to wash. With his clothes draped across her arm, she tiptoed and placed a kiss to his cheek.

"I'll be waiting for you to wake." She leveled her stance and met his silenced eyes. Though she wasn't sure if he heard, she continued anyway. "Rest. You're going to need it for your next lesson."

Caledonia closed the shed doors tight and made sure she locked them. A strange nagging at the base of her brain suggested it was best to weigh on the side of caution. After a long steady gaze across the loch at the wooded area, she issued a silent prayer for Struan's safety. The person in those woods yesterday probably was just a hiker; she tried to convince herself, yet it didn't still the growing suspicion in her gut. She tugged the door one more time before turning and heading into the house.

Fatigue filled her muscles. She desperately needed a nap. Struan's eagerness to learn made her smile. The bout of making out in the shed had her emotions frazzled. Where was this headed relationship wise? Could they remain friends after that show of heated affection towards one another? God, she wanted more of him. She wanted all he had to offer. Caledonia couldn't think straight. She needed to stop thinking about sex and Struan. It wasn't good.

At the door, she stared over her shoulder at the shed. Nothing would be decided at that moment. She sighed heavily. If nothing else, she had him in her life for a few more days before he'd return home.

Chapter Eight

He hated the fact he could not touch her. He'd wanted to kiss her and continue to ravish her mouth with the passion the dive created in his soul. Time played against them. Silently he prayed he'd placed enough distance between them that she had not turned to stone as well. Though he couldn't be sure, he took no chance that contact led to participation in the curse. Caledonia imprisoned in stone because of his overzealousness would not do. Not in his book. She deserved to suffer no part of this hideous daily transformation.

Damn this curse. Anger ravaged him with the desperate desire to rip Hume MacGillivray apart. If not for him, Struan would be free to pursue Caledonia and the phenomenal world of diving. If not for him… Struan's train of thought halted.

If not for the curse, he never would've been given the opportunity he has now. To dive and explore the loch at greater depths than his lungs ever carried him. By some obscure definition he should be thanking MacGillivray. Though no sound left his lips, the sensation of laughter filtered through his entombed soul. His eyes may not see and his body was frozen, but his mind was wide-awake with vivid images of his time spent beneath the water's surface with Caledonia.

She'd given him a present unlike any other. The world she opened for him brought sheer joy and wonderment to his entire being. Not to mention, dressed in the thing she called a diving suit did nothing to hide her curves. He liked the way the soft black material molded to her breasts and cupped them in a gentle caress. And her arse. *Och*, thinking about it was painful, especially frozen with no way to react to the beautiful vision swimming behind his eyes.

When she took the lead during their dive, he had been dumbstruck. Those solid round globes teased him with each motion of her legs propelling her through the water. Up, down. Up, down. It implanted images of him being buried deep within her, riding her. His shaft had reacted. It hardened and became painful in the tight fit of the suit he had worn. Each time they made contact, be it intentional or by accident, it didn't help alleviate his condition in the slightest. Instead it had intensified the ache in his bawls.

Reliving his first diving experience made him hunger for Caledonia, again. Though his body did not maintain the capability to react at that moment, he knew if he were in man form and not statue, his shaft would be at full attention and Caledonia would still be in his arms. At least, that is how he imagined it would be. The memory of her hand on his cock brought joy to his soul. It caught him off guard when she'd touched him.

A bold move on her part that he found exciting and made him want her even more. The one thing he wished, that they had been naked while exploring each other. The diving suit hid nothing, but it prevented actual skin-to-skin contact, which he craved.

A thought sparked through his head. Did his body remain in its excited state while frozen? If his eyes could roll, he knew they would. *Och.* Frozen with his shaft upright and wanton. Since there was no way to tell his condition, he internally shrugged it off. It didn't matter. Only Caledonia mattered.

With nothing else to do, he let his imagination guide him into a world of relaxed bliss. Diving with Caledonia, spending hours exploring the waters only to surface and spend the rest of the night tasting and discovering each other. *Och,* what a fine mess he was in. Caught between a rock and a hard place—literally.

* * * * *

The O'Reillys took the news better than she ever could've imagined. They didn't tease or call her daft when she explained about the statue. In reality, she'd had no choice. They'd returned while she slept and found the statue in a totally different state than when they left. It helped when Poppa and Momma both backed her word as truth. Not that it was necessary. Able and Percy had no reason not to trust Caledonia.

As Percy put it, "They knew she was a bit off-kilter in her thinking from time to time, but she'd never steered them down a path that didn't lead to an exciting adventure. And this was just another one of those *Caledonia adventures* as far as they were concerned."

According to Able, "If you didn't believe in supernatural things, then you shouldn't hang with Caledonia. Remember that banshee when we were kids? Knew then life with you'd never be boring."

A smile tickled her lips as she stood in the shower rethinking their earlier conversation. She couldn't have been blessed with a better pair of brothers even if her parents had spawned them. They both promised to help with Struan's dive training. And with them present, maybe it'd help curb that blasted sexual desire that ignited every time Struan even looked her way. Caledonia leaned into the water's hot stream, letting it soak her face. Never had it been this difficult for her to concentrate on something other than sex, especially while diving.

She turned the water colder and forced herself to stand in its direct flow. Full stream with cold-as-ice temperature didn't tinge the heat within her for more than just a sample of Struan's passion. Unable to absorb any more without catching a cold, she shut off the water and stepped out of the shower. With the towel in her hand, Caledoina dried herself. Images of Struan danced behind her eyes, toying with her overactive imagination.

Eyes closed, it was him drying her body, not her. The brush of the cotton across her nipples nearly made her moan but she bit it back, not wanting her folks to hear and knock on the door thinking something was wrong. Caledonia snapped out of her horny stupor, quickly dried and dressed. Something had to give before she burst. She shook herself over the adolescent sensations warping her ability to think straight. An adult woman maintained more control over her libido. She lifted her gaze to the mirror and mentally asked, *Didn't they?*

Caledonia left the bathroom and headed downstairs. It was almost time for Struan to be released. Her insides tumbled. How would he react to the O'Reillys? Would they get along? God, she hoped they'd at least tolerate each other. She stopped in the kitchen long enough to grab a fresh-baked scone and cup of hot tea. With them in hand, she held the door for her new best friend, the kitten Streak, who followed her to the shed. It surprised her earlier to find him asleep beside her on her pillow. He must've clawed his way up the comforter to get onto the bed. That feat alone amazed her.

Percy, Able and Poppa were aboard the boat making ready for another night of diving when she reached the dock. She waved.

"Hey, Caledonia," Percy called out as he jumped down on the dock. Streak didn't like it and hissed at him from behind Caledonia's ankles.

"I see one o' the litter has taken a liking to you," Poppa stated with a nod.

"Aye," Caledonia replied. With the scone eaten, she knelt and scooped him up, cuddling him close to her chest in one hand while holding her tea in the other. "I've named him Streak. Thought it was about time we had a mascot for the boat. What do you think?"

Poppa harrumphed good-naturedly. He took the kitten she handed him. After a moment of sizing him up, Poppa put him down on the boat and stated, "He'll do." He cocked an eyebrow at Caledonia and added in a stern yet teasing tone, "The moment he lays a tooth in one o' my hard-earned catches, he's bait."

Caledonia nearly snorted her tea, knowing her poppa wasn't capable of hurting an innocent being, especially a kitten.

"You wouldn't dare," the voice of her momma came from behind her, making her look over her shoulder. Aileen Kavanagh stood with her arms crossed over her chest and a steady glare, which contained a hint of humor, leveled on her poppa. On the ground beside her sat a large picnic basket and a cooler.

Caledonia swallowed her smile. The kitten was safe even if he was never in any real danger to begin with. Poppa harrumphed, waving his hands in defeat in the air then returned to rigging his gear for a night of fishing while they dove. She left the matter in good hands as she walked to the shed.

Sunlight clung by its last threads in the sky and she didn't want to miss Struan's moment of wakening. She opened the door, stepped inside. Because of the strange feeling of being watched from the woods the day before, she closed the door behind her. What happened in this shed, stayed in this shed.

She knew the moment of his freedom. Heat coated her flesh. The air sizzled with energy, setting the hairs on her arms and the back of her neck on end. It was a sign she associated with Struan's impending release. She couldn't help but smile when the flash of light appeared followed by his gorgeous face.

"Welcome back, bright eyes," Caledonia said with a smile.

"Caledonia," he gasped on a thicker-than-normal brogue as he stepped toward her and swept her into his arms.

He kissed her. She instantly responded. Caledonia parted her lips and granted him access. She hungered for Struan's kiss. Not like the first one they'd shared where he'd simply attacked her mouth or the sexually charged others from last night. This kiss was different. This kiss curled her toes. This kiss relayed his passion with each second it lasted. When they separated, she was breathless. Damn, the man knew how to kiss.

She leaned back in his arms, enjoying the closeness. The look of lust in his eyes lit her soul on fire with unadulterated need. If others weren't waiting for them, she'd peel him out of that suit and show him how badly she wanted him. A light knock reminded her that would have to wait. She closed her eyes, unable to believe her family's timing.

"Hey, Caledonia, is he awake? We want to meet him," Able called through the door.

"Yeah, don't keep him all to yourself. Share," Percy added and she couldn't miss the implication in his tone. Geez, those guys never quit.

In a low tone, she asked as she held his ardent gaze, "Are you ready to meet the O'Reillys? Remember, they may not be blood but we're as close as any sister and brother."

"I'll keep that in mind," he replied, releasing her.

Caledonia turned, walked to the door and switched on the light. She took a breath, knowing once she opened it private time with Struan wouldn't exist. Slowly she let them in then secured the door behind them.

"Struan, these two are my closest friends, Percy and Able O'Reilly." She turned to find for the first time in her life, neither had a voice. They stared wide-eyed at Struan. They circled him as if not sure they believed what they saw and looked for a flaw to prove it was some sort of trick.

"Gentlemen, I am Struan MacKinnon o' Clan MacKinnon," Struan spoke, holding out his hand, waiting for either of them to take it. Neither did.

They simply took a stance in front of him, arms crossed over their chests, shoulders back, spines straight. Struan lowered his hand. She noticed he appeared relaxed yet subtly readied his stance for a possible assault. Great, the room suddenly shrank around her with an overabundance of testosterone, thickening the air. Right before she jumped in to end it, Percy broke the silence.

"So you want to learn to dive."

"Aye. Caledonia took me for my first lesson last night."

"And you liked it?" Able asked without relaxing his stance.

"Aye."

"What are your intentions toward our Caledonia?" Percy's question floored her. Her expression did nothing to hide her surprise, especially with her mouth dangling wide open. Luckily for Percy, anger controlled her words and strangled them in her throat. Before she found the power to push them forth, Struan handled the situation with an expert's degree of delicacy.

"My intentions at the moment are to learn to dive. As for the future…" He gathered her hand in his and lifted it to brush a delicate kiss across her knuckles then leveled a non-challenging gaze upon the brothers. "We shall see what the fates decide."

Combined with the tender brush of his lips to her flesh, the words eased her anger at Percy for asking Struan's intentions. It really wasn't any of his business, but she should've expected he'd act like an overprotective brother. Did Struan mean what he said? His tender clasp of her hand twisted her insides, making it difficult to focus. Caledonia lifted her gaze to the O'Reillys and hoped for the best.

The brothers looked at one another. In a show of unspoken acceptance, they nodded then turned their attention back to Struan. Percy extended his hand. "Welcome, Struan. Let's get you on the boat and out to deeper waters. Caledonia tells us you want to visit the spot where we found you."

Caledonia breathed a sigh of relief. They accepted Struan. Now with that hurdle crossed, maybe they could get on with the night's dive plan. She released his hand and placed a gap between them. What she needed was a little bit of distance between him and her if she were to gain any control over the explicitly sexual thoughts gripping her brain. *Think dive. Think dive.*

Struan took his hand and then shook Able's as he said, "That is my goal before I return home to Castle MacKinnon."

"Whenever you're ready, we'll cast off and head for deeper waters," Able stated. He nodded toward Caledonia. "Your Momma made us a fine basket of food and filled a cooler full of refreshments so we're set for most of the night."

"If'n you don't mind, I would like to take a moment to freshen up a wee bit before I spend another night in this suit," he replied as he tugged at the neckline.

"We understand that one. Being in a dive suit too long can be restrictive," Percy agreed.

"Take as long as you need. We'll be down on the dock when you're ready," Able added as he nudged Percy and headed for the door.

"Here, let me help you with that zipper," Caledonia said, standing behind him. She reached for the zip cord and tugged it downward. Inch by inch, perfectly muscled flesh appeared, stilling the breath in her lungs.

Nothing on earth could have pulled her eyes away as Struan peeled the neoprene from his body. The scent of his last dive coated his gorgeous male form. A light sheen of sweat mixed with the essence of the loch stirred her desire from a low simmer to a high boil. This was torture. Her hands shook. Her insides hummed. Desire threatened to take control, but the O'Reillys were waiting so she refused to allow it. Caledonia released the cord and quickly moved toward the door.

Without looking back, she called over her shoulder, "Hang the dive suit on the hook on the wall then come up to the house. I'll prepare the bathroom for you to take a shower."

The cool evening air slapped her in the face but did nothing to knock sense into her overactive sex drive. She managed to stare straight ahead as she scooted across the lawn to the house. In the bathroom, she laid out a fresh towel and washcloth, made sure there was enough soap and shampoo then returned to the kitchen. He entered just as she took the last step.

The dark-blue diving swim trunks hid nothing. Caledonia's mouth dried at the impressive lump in the tight-knit fabric. Damn. He was one fine man. Caledonia darted her eyes up the length of his muscled torso to land on the molten-hot gaze within those deep-sea blues. It took several seconds before she noticed he held a bag in his hand.

"W-What—"she stammered. "What's in the bag?"

"Percy and Able loaned me a fresh pair o' swim trunks and a what they call a t-shirt. My kilt and shirt seem to have gone missing."

"They're not missing," Caledonia said, turning toward the table. She lifted the clean, folded clothes and held them out to him. "I washed them."

"Thank you," he replied, taking them from her and setting them back on the table. "I greatly appreciate your kindness, but I won't be needing them until later."

He nodded then walked toward the stairs.

"Do you remember how everything works in the bathroom?" she asked.

"Aye, milady," he answered, shooting her a coy smile across his shoulder. "If I have any concerns on how things operate, I will call for your assistance."

Her cheeks flushed and brought a smile to his lips. The function of the modern bathroom had been described to him in detail on his first night of release, when he asked where he might relieve himself. Now he was anxious to freshen. Personal cleanliness ranked high on his agenda. Though he had spent the night in the water with Caledonia and knew he was clean, he felt itchy from being frozen in stone wrapped in neoprene as she had called it.

It took him a few minutes to work through the steps of running the water. Turning knobs to maintain the perfect temperature amazed him. Even though he'd done it before, he stooped and looked under the sink for a hidden heat source. Again there was no fire. Struan straightened. Now that he mastered the art of the sink, he turned to the shower.

A few adjustments and the water felt comfortable to the touch. He shed the trunks and stepped into the shower. Percy was right. A hot shower and the itchiness disappeared. He soaped from head to toe with the fresh-scented soap, rinsed, then simply stood in the steady stream for a few moments. The constant pulse to his neck, shoulders and back put images in his head of delicate fingers swirling and kneading his flesh.

He imagined Caledonia's fingers caressed him, sparking his desire to life. Her lips touched his in a delicate invitation then retreated, leaving him hungry for a sample of her flavor. Involuntarily, he leaned forward as if chasing after her mouth. Water pelted his face.

Struan's eyes flew wide open. He shut the water off and stepped out, staring at the empty stall. Never had anything tickled his senses as the magic of this shower. It not only cleaned and relaxed him, it led his mind to think of the one thing that kept him sane during his day of imprisonment. Caledonia.

Och. His bawls ached with need for that lovely lady. Struan toweled dry and did his best to think of things less enticing than Caledonia. It wasn't until he fought with the clean swim trunks that he managed to set aside his thoughts of lust and wondered just how men's shafts survived such snug clothing. He pulled the t-shirt Able loaned him on over his head like it had been explained and straightened it. Again, a taut fit. Struan tugged at the neckline, flexed his shoulders and arms in an attempt to stretch the fabric. It helped a little but not much.

He gathered the dirty suit and towel then bounded down the stairs. Meeting Aileen in the kitchen, she took the items and directed him to meet the others down on the dock. Struan grabbed his clothes off the table. She handed him a scone and scooted him out the door. After he put his clothes in the shed, he joined the others on the boat and they shoved off for deeper waters.

"Tonight," Caledonia announced as she turned to face him. "We're going to at least fifty feet. Think you can handle it?"

The breeze fluttered a few escapees from her braid to frame her face. The sight of her dressed in a diving suit with her curves accentuated, stirred his shaft. He knew if he didn't do something soon, all would know just how much he wanted Caledonia.

"Aye," he replied right before he peeled off the shirt and quickly busied himself with the diving suit Percy handed him. He arched an eyebrow and leveled a playful gaze her way. "I can handle anything you have for me."

His innuendo didn't go unnoticed by Caledonia. The heat in his eyes confirmed what she thought she'd heard in his tone. When he'd gone to take a shower, every ounce of her wanted to follow him up the stairs. *To make sure he was okay, not to join him.* She'd battled with her conscience before taking the chicken's way out and leaving the house entirely before she did something stupid.

Then the sight of him casually strolling across the yard to the dock had nearly stopped her heart. The man truly looked good in swim trunks and a t-shirt. Silently she prayed for the strength to keep her hands to herself and teach him to dive. He had a goal he wanted to reach before he returned home and she promised to help him. When he bent over in front of her, stepped into the dive suit and did a little wiggle as he pulled it up, it was all she could do not to drop her jaw and drool. She spun around.

Lord help her. The best she could hope for was that the water was extra cold tonight. She doubted even a day of sitting in a barrel of solid ice would take the edge off the razor-sharp need cutting through her for Struan at that moment. She'd thought of nothing but him all day. And she hoped their little sampling of each other earlier was only the beginning. Caledonia double and triple checked the equipment while the others dressed for the dive. When they reached the spot she'd suggested for their venture, Poppa cut the engine and weighed anchor.

As soon as they were ready, all four went over the side. When her eyes adjusted, it amazed her how well Struan did. He took to diving like a master. She hung back and took it all in, keeping close to the group while enjoying the sight of Struan exploring the underworld with the giddy excitement of a child with a new toy. With Percy's and Able's help, she managed to take him to the fifty-foot mark without difficulty. They worked as a team leading, guiding and teaching. A couple of times, she even noted a bit of horseplay. Boys. She sighed and shook her head.

It tore at her heart to motion time to surface was near. Struan swam beside her, took her hand then laid something in her palm. She aimed the light so she could see. It sparkled slightly. It was the oddest rock she'd ever seen. When she looked back at him, she swore he smiled around his regulator. She nodded then made the signal again that it was time to surface. She tucked it into the pouch she kept at her waist for trinkets and treasures she might find along the way. When she took the lead he followed, as did Percy and Able.

They broke the surface after an hour of diving. Percy and Able were the first out of the water. Struan swam close to Caledonia. As they bobbed in the water, he smiled at her. The mask sat on top of his head. His regulator hung from his shoulder. He looked the picture-perfect part of a diver on a sports magazine.

Caledonia wanted nothing more than to kiss him, but refrained when Percy reached over the edge to take her fins and helped her up the ladder. Struan followed. He fit right in with the O'Reillys. They showed him how to stow the gear and check for damage. As per their dive plan, they reasoned it would be best for Struan to take him down deeper in increments. Two dives tonight. One at fifty feet, the second at sixty and see how he did.

While Percy and Able kept him busy, she slipped the rock out of her pouch and held it to the light. It was oddly shaped. Smooth on one side and rough on the other, but pretty. She looked over at Struan who stared across Percy's shoulder at her. She couldn't help but smile. When Percy pointed something out to him on the dive chart in his hand, Struan's gaze fell from hers to the chart, but not before it left a warm glow inside her. Yeah, the man was perfect even if he was over two hundred years old.

They ate, rested, played with the kitten and fished for several hours before they moved to deeper waters for the last dive of the night. It went well. Struan did phenomenal. At the rate he was learning and adapting to the water depths and pressures, she didn't doubt his abilities to take on extreme depth with the proper diving education. Was he willing to wait and take it in the slow increments she knew were necessary to build his skills?

The question gnawed at her the entire way back to the dock. Excitement flowed off him with every dive. She watched him interact with Percy, Able and her poppa as if they were lifelong pals. It warmed her heart. But it saddened her as well. Once they reached the bottom and he made his peace, would he be gone? When he looked her way and smiled, she returned the smile. It was wrong to want more. But she did.

They docked and helped load the scuba tanks into the van for Poppa to take in the morning for refilling. Struan and Caledonia lingered, sitting on the end of the dock after the O'Reillys left for home and Poppa went to bed, taking the kitten to the house with him. Side by side, they quietly looked out over the loch, taking in the silence of the late night hour.

Struan's hand wheedled its way into hers. He lifted it to his lips and pressed a gentle kiss across her knuckles. "I meant what I said, Caledonia. You have given me a precious gift by teaching me to dive. It is one o' which I can never repay."

"You don't have to repay me anything, Struan. It's my pleasure."

His eyebrow arched and a mischievous look crossed his face. "Your pleasure is teaching me?"

"Aye."

He leaned in closer, tipped her chin and on a husky breath whispered, "Pleasure comes in many forms. One is in a kiss."

Slow and delicate, he tasted her lips. He slid an arm around her waist and held her close. He captured her mouth in a passionate kiss. He delved into the wondrous flavor of Caledonia's mouth—rich, feminine with a hint of sugar 'n' spice. One hand held her in an embrace while the other released her braid.

Thick, dark strands twisted in his fingers as he combed through her hair, loosening the last weave to flow along her back and fall below her waist. He let its soft texture slowly drift from his fingertips only to stroke his hand through its length again. The sensation in his palm as he caressed its silkiness from shoulder to the enticing curve of her bottom, sent an image to his brain he couldn't deny. He wanted her, to have her ride him using her hair to shield them in a curtain of deep, dark silk as they fulfilled each other's desires.

Struan broke from the kiss. Placing his forehead to hers, he inhaled. A mixture of the loch and pure woman combined and gave him the perfect aroma he'd forever associate with being Caledonia.

"Caledonia," he whispered. "I've thought o' nothing but you while I lay cursed."

The brush of her hand to the front of his swim trunks made his hardened shaft twitch. He met her ardent gaze and prayed he read her right. She wrapped her arms around his neck and attacked his mouth in the hottest kiss he'd ever experienced. Without breaking the connection, he lifted her as he stood. Her legs hugged his waist as he carried her to the shed. One arm held her tight while the other closed the door behind them. Caledonia flicked on the light with her foot as they entered.

For every kiss he placed upon her, she matched it hot and hurriedly. She released his neck and worked her cover-up over her head. Struan nipped at her left breast through her swimsuit and suckled the pointy tip into his mouth. Her gasp fueled his desire. He grabbed the material in his teeth and tugged. Caledonia squirmed until she worked the straps off her shoulders and down her arms, freeing her breasts for his delight.

He suckled from one glorious breast to the other, nipping and tugging until both nipples were reddened buds. Each tender bite to her flesh garnered him a sensual wiggle of her against his shaft, increasing his need to be inside her. The grip of her legs around his hips tightened with every tug of her nipple deep into his mouth. Though she'd warned against it earlier, he sensed she liked a bit o' roughness in her bed.

Struan swiped the table clear with one arm while still ravishing her breast and holding on to her. He laid her on the table. Her legs lingered loosely around his hips. Her breasts rose and fell with each heavy intake of air in a teasing dance that watered his mouth. He grabbed the swimsuit and peeled it down her luxurious body.

Now nothing prevented him from plundering her treasure. He stood between her legs, enjoying the view. Moist, pink flesh beckoned. The sight of not one hair intrigued him. Shaven clean. His shaft twitched and his bawls tightened. Never had he seen such. His urgency catapulted to its highest level. With the speed and ease of a skilled warrior, he skimmed those swim trunks off to pool around his ankles.

Struan grabbed her hips and slid her to the table's edge. No delicacy came into play. He breached her opening and paused only for a second, giving her that moment to conform to his size. The heat of her gaze raked over him. Her nails scraped gently down his abdomen and he sensed he'd entered a woman who knew what she wanted. The dig of her heels into the back of his thighs granted him farther entrance. He slid an arm under her waist and lifted her without much of an effort, seating her perfectly.

Caledonia released a loud groan of ecstasy. She grasped his shoulders and her legs tightened around his waist. When she wiggled, he knew he was right. He'd found a true *fiadh-cat* to warm his bed, especially when her nails raked across his shoulders and she bit his lower lip, playfully without breaking the skin. It set his soul on fire.

He spun around and used the wall as leverage. Harder and deeper he plunged into her until her juices soaked the upper flesh of his thighs. Wet 'n' wild, perfect for him. He matched her stroke for solid stroke. He wrestled from one breast to the other, tugging, sucking and teasing the tip and well-rounded mounds. He liked the sounds Caledonia made, especially when he entered bawls-deep as he bit her nipple in a tight, yet tender tug. She was not a silent lover, but one whose gasps and groans fanned the flames of his desire and drove their coupling into a wicked, fast, hard pace.

Feeling her inner muscles tighten around him, he sensed her release neared. He cupped the back of her head and captured her mouth in a rough, passionate kiss. Pounding into her, he sent her over the edge. She groaned into his mouth as her sheath clenched and her legs locked tightly around his waist. Her nails dug into the back of his shoulders to the point he sensed he'd lost some flesh, but didn't care. It added to his urgent need for release.

Yet, he stopped.

He fisted his hand in her hair and gently separated from their kiss. Her wild-eyed look thrilled him to the core. It was all he could do to hold on for one second more. He wanted to show her who ruled this moment of pleasure. He wanted her to know tonight would not be their last.

"Caledonia, you are my *fiadh-cat*, my *fèilleil fiadh boireannach*." He kissed her tenderly, then glided back until only the thick head of his cock remained. "My *fèilleil fiadh-cat* and no one else's."

Struan entered Caledonia, hard and swift. Though he tried, he could no longer prevent his release. Her heat gloved him, wrapped him tight and pushed him toward orgasm. Several bawls-deep plunges and he was lost. He buried his face in her hair as he spent his seed inside her. Breathing in, the scent of roses mixed with a rich womanly essence filled his nose. Caledonia was the closest thing to heaven he'd ever found.

The way Struan had looked at her under the moonlit sky had speared her heart. Sadness and a longing for an irretrievable era shone in his expression. Caledonia had wanted to touch him, to hold him, to soothe his despair. That's what she'd truly meant to do, befriend him. Lust had gotten the better of her. She licked her lips shakily, tasting the flavor that belonged solely to Struan. He twitched inside her and she desperately wanted to stay wrapped like this forever.

He nuzzled her neck, her hair and simply held her steady in his arms with the wall against her back. It amazed her that this man lifted her as if she weighed nothing. When he'd carried her from the dock, she'd noticed then it hadn't winded him in the least. His breath never became heavy until he fucked her up against the wall. Just the thought sent a chill of pure joy down her spine to pool in her pelvis. God, she wanted him again.

What was wrong with her?

She leaned her head back, eyes closed, relishing the sensations still rippling through her core. Something about Struan got her hot in an instant and made her hunger for sex, rough and wild. A way she'd never experienced. The image of him dressed in neoprene, hot and sexy deep beneath the water's surface, flashed behind her eyes.

Eyes opened, the sight of ripped, muscled male had her fingers itching to touch. Not an ounce of fat entered the picture. The man had a perfect chest, washboard abs most body builders would die for and a set of arms that felt good wrapped around her. His massive size made her feel small and petite in his presence.

When the swim trunks had hit the floor, her heart skipped. Between a solid set of thighs was a healthy portion of cock pointed straight at her. She'd wanted to fuck him and she'd gotten her wish. His whispered words in ancient Gaelic etched themselves for eternity inside her brain. The way he spoke them in his native tongue rolled on a deep Scottish brogue had made her even wetter. She recognized several words he'd spoken. A few of them she didn't understand, but intended to unravel their meaning.

Caledonia shifted and hoped he remained resting inside of her. She liked the sensation of total fullness. It was something she'd never experienced with Kip. She shook that unwanted image from her head. Kip was the past. This gorgeous hunk between her thighs was the present and she intended to enjoy every possible minute. Even though the little voice of conscience whispered it was wrong. *What was wrong with sharing pleasurable sex with this Scottish God of a man?* Nothing, she decided. Not as long as she helped him find his way in this new place and time.

She gathered his face in her hands and smiled as their gazes met.

"Struan," she said on a shaky voice. She paused and gathered her resolve. Did she truly want to know what he'd said? What if he'd called her some sort of whore? She shook that thought off and asked, "What did you say? I'm not well-versed in the ancient tongue."

His smile broadened and heated her insides. The man had a gorgeous smile and a set of the deepest sea-blue eyes she'd ever seen. Running her fingers through his hair, loosening his ponytail, she noted the rich, red highlights mixed within his dark black shade and its length fell to between his broad shoulders. He was a hairdresser's dream, yet his was truly natural. The touch of his fingertips to her chin made her lift her gaze to his again. The look in his eyes softened.

"You are my wildcat, my beautiful wild woman. My beautiful wildcat and no one else's."

Her heart expanded. He'd called her *his* wildcat, *his* beautiful wild woman. No one had ever said such to her and it thrilled her, but she wasn't sure she liked the possessive overtone of his use of *and no one else's*. She was not a possession to be owned. This was something she needed to make clear. Women of his time may have been objects, but she intended to make it known women of this time were individuals, not property. Looking at him, the passionate heat in his gaze gave her pause in her decision. Maybe right now wasn't the time for a battle of the sexes. Not while they both lingered in the afterglow.

Struan kissed her tenderly as he guided her to stand. Her legs trembled and she had to concentrate to remain upright and not crumble to the floor. The slide of him from within her left an emptiness she didn't like. She snuggled closer to him. His softened cock nestled against her abdomen and she swore it twitched as if it tried to harden again. If he managed that, it would be an impressive feat. She bit back the urge to giggle. In her limited experience, it was her understanding men didn't recover as quickly as women.

Both breasts pressed into the rock wall of his chest. She enjoyed the sensation of flesh on flesh, hers soft and pliable, his hard and enjoyable, which stimulated her nipples to remain stiff through the simple connection. Standing in his arms, she noted his height to be at least six foot since she had to tilt her chin to meet his gaze. At five-five, she didn't consider herself to be a tall woman, but she wasn't short either.

A low rumble rose to her ears and gave evidence he represented a typical man. Sex first, food second. She leaned back and met his gaze. "You're hungry. Get dressed and we'll go to the house. I'm sure I can find you something to eat."

Caledonia stepped away from him. He grabbed his kilt. Struan's fluidity in dressing, muscles bunched and flexed, reminded her the loss was worth it. A smile crossed her lips she doubted would disappear for some time.

When she bent to pick up her swimsuit cover-up, a thick arm snaked around her waist and tugged her tight to him. She gasped. The solid rod beneath his kilt could not be mistaken pressed against her bottom. It surprised her he was hard again. The heat of him cocooned her as he leaned over, chest against her back, and boldly said, his voice husky and deep, "This is the position I wish to take you in, next time we share intimacies." The tip of his tongue brushed her ear ever so lightly, driving a spike of pure need to her core. "You have a fine arse, my *fiadh-cat*."

He released her as quickly as he'd grabbed her, slapping her ass with a commanding open palm that set her off-balance. She involuntarily stepped forward to keep from falling. Her ass cheek stung but her clit hummed with need. Never had something like that ever thrilled her or ignited her curiosity as his words and actions.

Caledonia righted herself. It took several deep breaths to calm the flood of electrified emotions powering through her system. Surprise. Anger. Desire. Purely physical need kept her moist and ready should he act upon his claim. Did she want him to? Caledonia slowly turned to face him. He stood tall and proud, handsome and rugged, the eyes of a sexual predator stared her way and her knees weakened.

Yeah, she instantly decided. She wanted him to take her anyway he so desired.

Chapter Nine

She closed her eyes the moment her head hit the pillow. Morning sun beamed through the bedroom window but she knew there was no way it would keep her awake. Not after the wonderful night she'd shared with Struan. They'd raided the kitchen in the early-morning hours then sat in the shed, talking until the curse interrupted the best date of her life.

Damn curse. She sighed heavily. A low meow caught her ears and she reached over the side and scooped Streak onto the bed. The memory of Struan playing with the kitten on the boat the night before teased her senses and made her lips twitch into a smile. Gentle to a fault, he'd held the tiny critter in his large hands and handled him with care.

Ummm, the perfect man filled her thoughts and lulled her into a deep sleep. Every ounce of her ached but in a good, totally satisfied way. Caledonia snuggled Streak closer and gave in to her desperate need to rest and recuperate.

* * * * *

Daytime was the best time to steal from a fishing village.

Most were on the water by daybreak, trying to eek out a living. Besides, he knew this house and the grounds well. He'd waited and watched for the exact moment to strike. Fin and Aileen Kavanagh left that morning in the van. Carefully, he searched the area. The O'Reillys were nowhere in sight. He snuck past the house on foot, carefully looking in the side windows. Caledonia was nowhere to be seen. Though his view was limited to mainly the kitchen, he decided the house was empty.

Where was she? He silently worked his way around the house. Seeing no one, he continued to the shed. Peering around the edge, he noted the boat was empty. He glanced across his shoulder toward the house. Could she possibly be in there? He stood stock sill and listened. No noise. No sounds of movement, no teakettle brewing. Where was Caledonia? This wasn't like her. Was she sleeping in? Was she sick?

He peered inside the window of the shed. The statue stood in the center of the room. Odd, it looked as if it had changed position, again. He shook it off. Eyes must be playing tricks. It didn't matter. He had a buyer and now all he needed was the merchandise.

No neighbors nearby made his task even easier. Even if someone saw him from the loch, by the time they got there, they'd be too late. The lock on the shed gave him no issues. He grinned. This was as easy as breathing. He motioned to the driver of his van to back in closer. The moment the van stopped, two huge goons he hired exited the rear. One pulled out a large hand truck from the cargo area. The other lowered the mechanical ramp at the rear of the van. Kip opened the double doors of the shed.

Sunlight filled the small room. Once his eyes adjusted on the statue, he was even more certain it looked as if it were positioned differently. A bit more upright and his hands were at its sides whereas before… Maybe he hadn't gotten as good a look as he thought. He shrugged. Either way it didn't matter.

The tidbit of news and slightly blurred picture he posted on an obscure, black-market antiquities loop had generated a decent amount of buzz about the find. Several interested parties contacted his private account with bids within hours of his upload. Substantial bids. He nodded as he circled the statue. The bidding would close this day and the bidder would be informed where to pick up his prize as soon as his money was deposited.

"Make sure you don't drop this," he stated as the hired muscle entered the shed.

"Won't be a problem," one of them replied in a gruff thick, brogue.

"Aye. Isn't as heavy as it looks," the other interjected as he tipped the statue for his buddy to slide the thin metal slat of the hand truck underneath.

"I don't care how heavy *or* light it is," Kip stated in a snippy tone. "I simply want it moved in one piece. It's no good to me in pieces."

"Not a problem, mate." The larger of the two huffed then completed the task of leaning the statue back into the cradle of the hand truck. While one held the hand truck steady, the other strapped the statue in place so it wouldn't slide or slip.

After a few minutes, they had loaded and secured the statue into the van.

"Ahhh," he sighed. He'd acquired his prize without a hitch and all before lunch.

* * * * *

The door slammed as the O'Reillys entered. Caledonia took the last step into the kitchen. Momma and Poppa sat at the table having a cup of tea and a bite to eat.

"Where'd Struan end up last night?" Percy asked.

"What do you mean?" Caledonia replied, hoping her cheeks didn't give away the events she'd shared with Struan. "He's in the shed."

"We unloaded the scuba tanks from the van to the shed," Able stated as he poured a cup of tea. "He's not there, lass. We were wondering where you hid him."

She shot out the door and across the yard. She yanked open the door and couldn't believe what she saw. Struan was gone. She spun around in a panic, searching the surrounding area for any signs of her Scottish laird. Percy, Able and Fin came around the corner of the shed just in time to see her pound the shed door with her fist and scream.

"Kip," she growled between clenched teeth. "That no-good son-of-a-bitch."

"I'll call the police. Won't take them but an hour or so to get here," Able said as he immediately spun around and headed toward the house.

"No," Caledonia gasped. Able froze and both he and his brother, slack-jawed, stared at her.

"Don't be telling me you've still got feelings for that sap." Percy's tone didn't hide his strong hatred for Kip.

"Oh hell no!" she snapped angrily. "It's not that—" Caledonia closed her mouth. What could she say? How much would her closest friends understand? She dared a moment's glance from one to the other before making her decision. These two were her brothers, if not by blood, by a lifetime of experiences both good and bad.

"Then what is it, Caledonia?" Percy asked. With his arms crossed over his chest, he leveled a direct stare that swirled with a mixture of angry undertones and confusion on her. She gained a similar look from Able.

Caledonia took a breath and began where she knew she should, at the beginning of when all the weird spirit stuff started in her life. "Do the two of you remember the time we ended up in that root cellar behind the castle when we were kids?"

Percy snickered then said, "You talking about when Able fell in and we had to fetch him out? Big scaredy cat o' the dark."

"Hey, I take offense to that. I was a wee lad," Able chimed in. His face flushed a light shade of red. Caledonia guessed he remembered how he cried until they lit a couple of makeshift brush torches and went in after him.

Caledonia nodded and cupped Able's cheek. "It's okay. We know you've outgrown that now. If it wasn't for you, I never would've found the riddle, which was written to save Struan."

Brows bunched and total confusion lined their expressions. Able asked, "What's that got to do with this? We need to call the police."

"You two took an oath and stood beside me then, when we agreed not to tell anyone about that banshee. You stood beside me when things went haywire at the Bermuda Triangle. We can't call the police. Think about it. He's an ancient Scotsman trapped by a curse in stone. What happens to him if he breaks free?" Caledonia looked from one to the other. "Who's going to believe him but us?"

"If he's got his sword on him, I say he kicks some arse." Percy's tone dripped with humor.

Caledonia shot a quick glance about the shed. "It looks as if he does have it. I don't see it."

Able's mouth opened but he didn't get the chance.

"Before either of you say another word," Fin stated point-blank. "I see where you're going here, Caledonia. If he wakes before we find him, the consequences could be disastrous. We have to find him without the police." Fin straightened and shot a glare from one to the other. "Within that block of stone beats the heart o' a Scotsman and we must find him and help him return home. Are you with us or not?"

The oversized, redheaded O'Reilly brothers looked at one another.

"What'd you think?" Able asked. "You up for hunting Kip and getting Struan back?"

"Depends." Percy looked at Caledonia. "Anything goes when we find him."

She nodded her acknowledgement, but he added, "That includes beating the snot out of him."

"Aye, but I get first punch," she replied with a shrug.

"We're in," Percy said. "You know, Able, we could never let Caledonia or old man Kavanagh down."

"Who you calling old, boy?" Fin harrumphed good-naturedly. "If we didn't have to find that good-for-nothing Kip, I'd show you there's a lot o' fire in me fists."

"Aye," Aileen interrupted as she came around the corner and hugged his waist. "And though I pray it doesn't come to a fist fight, we might need that fire to save Struan. So save the flames for that and don't be wasting them on the boys, dear."

Fin turned into her hug. Over his shoulder, he cockily teased. "You two are saved by a woman, *again*."

Caledonia shook her head. She had to give it to Poppa. He knew just how to handle the O'Reilly brothers. He'd been their surrogate dad ever since their father was killed in a tragic industrial fishing accident when they were eight.

"What say you to us finding out which direction Kip took off in and beating the shite out o' him?" Able's comment surprised Caledonia. He wasn't normally the one to start the fight. Granted he wouldn't walk away once one was underway, but it wasn't like him to make the suggestion outright. And now this was twice within about a week's time he'd offered to knock some sense into Kip.

"I'm hoping finding him won't be a problem," Caledonia said as she turned and headed for the house. "But catching him before he sells Struan to some black-market collector might be. We've got to act fast."

"Don't fret, dear." Momma fell in step at her side. "When night falls, the situation may right itself on its own."

She crossed the threshold and did a mad dash upstairs to her room. One thing she knew about Kip—he was predictable. There were a handful of web sites she was aware he frequented. Whenever she located a valuable artifact, he jumped online quicker than she could blink and started a bidding war with some rather undesirable people in her opinion. It tore her heart apart to think of where a specific few rare objects of history landed because of Kip's greed.

Her teeth gritted and her jaw tightened as she shook the image of what she wanted to do to Kip from her head. Law no longer allowed disembowelment, but Struan didn't know that. If he woke and found he'd been stolen and sold like a trinket, would he react like the warrior she suspected him to be? Though she hated Kip, she knew she had to find Struan before nightfall. This battle wasn't between him and

Kip. It was hers and hers alone to fight. She thought it ended when he won just about everything in the divorce. Guess he didn't know when to cut his losses and leave her alone.

Returning to the kitchen with her laptop, Caledonia took a seat at the table. Poppa spoke on the phone in the next room. Momma set a cup of tea beside the computer as she booted up.

"Who's Poppa talking to?"

"He's setting off the barkin' chain," Momma quipped and Caledonia laughed. It'd been years since she'd heard that term, which usually Poppa used for Momma when she gossiped with her lady friends via telephone. "He's making sure everyone he knows tells everyone they know that the diving shed was broken into and a valuable asset was stolen. That way, if anyone saw something odd today, it'll get back to him and maybe help with finding Struan."

"Where are the O'Reillys?"

"Patricia came home from visiting with her sister. They walked home to borrow their mom's car so we can split up and go out looking. They're guessing Kip had to be in a van to cart Struan out o' here."

"Since Mrs. O'Reilly is home, does that mean her sister is on the mend?" Caledonia asked.

"Aye." Her mother nodded.

"That's good to hear."

She took a sip of her tea and typed on the keyboard with the fingers of one hand. One click and the file she kept on Kip's special auction sites popped into view and opened. He didn't know she had this information. Unfortunately, she'd stumbled upon it by accident after their divorce was final. He'd left the office of Marine Treasures Salvage with a window open on his computer while she was there cleaning out the few items she won.

Good conscience tried to talk her out of attaching the zip drive that was in her pile of office materials, but the agony of being defeated in court controlled her hand. She plugged it in and downloaded copies of almost everything he wouldn't want known about him in the proper world of antiquities. It would probably cost him the company, if she had the money to drag him back to court and provide what she'd learned as evidence. Caledonia sat back, set the tea down and skimmed the lists of sites. Lucky he was so damn anal. They were not only alphabetical, but also listed by what interested certain collectors.

She visited site after site, looking for anything that would lead her to Struan. Kip wouldn't let a prize statue simply sit in storage. No, he had to have a bidding event going on somewhere. Determination made her fingers fly on the keyboard until she struck gold.

"Bingo," she squealed.

The screen door flapped shut behind the O'Reillys entering the kitchen. Percy inquired, "I take it our timing couldn't be better."

"Nope, it couldn't." She glanced at the clock. "We've got less than three hours until dusk. The moment night falls, Struan will wake. That alone should scare the shite out o' Kip. But I doubt he managed to carry Struan's statue alone. He had help. No telling who or what sort o' thugs he's hired."

"You leave the thugs to us," Able replied. Both he and his brother straightened, biceps flexed, fists at the ready. Their eyes shined with the hunger for a good fight. "Been awhile since me and Percy had a good row."

"Aye, way too long," Percy concurred with a nod.

"Okay," Poppa said as he hung up the phone after making more than a dozen calls. "Seems Mrs. Potter passed a van around noon. It turned off the main road and onto our lane. Since it looked similar to our van, she thought nothing o' it. Silas was walking to the pub about a half hour later and said a van passed him. It was headed toward the A9."

"Good work, Poppa," Caledonia praised. "With that, it confirms the information I found concerning a specific auction." She waved her hand excitedly, motioning for them to gather around her laptop. She pointed out the ongoing bidding war between two individuals. "It appears as if Struan's quite popular."

"You sure this is about our friend?"

"Aye." She scrolled to the top of the page and there sat the evidence. A perfect picture of Struan as she'd left him this morning. Kip must've snapped that with his phone and uploaded it to the site before he left the shed. What a dumbarse! She zoomed in on the background and proved her theory. On the wall behind it hung her diving gear complete with her initials. Proof enough to get him arrested if it had to go that far.

"Hey, isn't that your—"

"That it is, Able. That it is," she replied.

"What a bawl juggler," Percy proclaimed. "Only an idiot would take a picture at the crime he just committed and post it on the web."

Caledonia clicked on a tab at the top. It listed an address she was familiar with as the pick-up location.

Yep, he truly was a dumb-arse.

Chapter Ten

Traffic stalled his progress and hampered his mood. A flipped truck and a five-car pile-up on the A9 stopped traffic for over an hour. Mobile Internet dead zones agitated him even more. First and foremost for a successful bidding war, he needed constant contact with his potential buyers. Sweat beaded his brow and anticipation knotted his gut when the van lurched and advanced three whole car lengths. Second most important, a swift close to the auction and a timely hand-off of the merchandise to the highest bidder.

The trick was not to get too greedy, he reminded himself. Last auction almost ended in disaster when he nearly got snagged in a police sting operation. The winner picked up their prize and he left with cash in hand just moments before a special police team encircled the empty warehouse where they'd met. He felt certain someone tipped them off. Kip sneered. Must have been that jealous bitch, Lillianna. Never should've hired her. Then again, she was a tight piece of ass. A slow smile twitched his lips as he stared ahead. Unfortunately, she demanded half of the profits and he fired her.

Kip checked the bars on his phone. Still no viable connection to the auction. Damn. He thrashed his head against the headrest of the passenger side seat in the van. He had one of the hottest items he'd ever acquired on auction and no way to check on its status.

Once past the traffic snarl, the trek to the storage facility in Edinburgh should be over long before dark. He shivered inwardly. He hated the thought of having to switch to using this location. It sat in an unsavory section of Edinburgh as far as he was concerned. For this little venture, it was more centrally located and easily accessible for all involved. Especially him. A short ferry ride from the port at Newhaven to Kirkcaldy and he'd board his salvage vessel, the *Spùinneadair-mara*, and set sail for a distant horizon, long before anyone caught wind of his misdeeds.

He glanced out of the corner of his eye at one of the individuals he hired for this salvage retrieval. A thin, gaunt sort-o-fellow with wire-rimmed glasses and a really bad comb-over, sat behind the wheel, steering through the maze of disaster marked off by cones, police and emergency vehicles.

He'd gotten no names and paid them half of the agreed-upon fee up front. The other half would be given the moment they safely placed the statue in the storage unit. Removal of the statue would be the purchaser's responsibility. A sigh of relief escaped as the van gained some speed.

For a second he thought of how marriage to Cali had cramped his style. That's why he let her go, Kip decided. Regrettably, one thing suffered with her loss, Marine Treasures Salvage's business declined. Not one major find since she left, Kip scoffed. Lillianna couldn't locate an artifact even if handed written instructions with specific directions to a sunken ship.

He hadn't intended to acquire such a worthy prize for auction on this trip. The main reason had been to convince Callie to work for him. Her refusal left him no other alternative. With her financial situation on the downward slope, he knew she had to have found something worthwhile or she wouldn't be diving the loch. He'd watched and waited. It paid off, at least for him.

Kip snickered. When would she ever learn, victory would always be his?

* * * * *

"Caledonia, I heard on the radio there's been a major accident on the A9 near Kinross," Percy spouted as she swung into the passenger seat of the van. "If we swing onto the back roads, we can make our way to the bridge in North Queensferry and bypass the whole mess. It'll put us in Edinburgh hopefully before Struan wakes."

"Whatever it takes. I trust your judgment on this." Caledonia turned her gaze to his. A smile teased her lips as his last two words penetrated her brain. "So, you really do believe in me?"

"Aye," Percy said, reached across the seat and touched her cheek. "You're the sister we never had, Caledonia. Family believes in family no matter how nuts you think their idea may be. You never know what might pan out, especially with you. We've learned the crazier the idea, the greater the adventure. You've made our lives interesting to say the least. It's why we love you and will do anything to protect you."

She choked back the tears that threatened to fall. Neither he nor Able ever said anything so sweet to her. Mostly it was brotherly torment and teasing that came out of their mouths. This took her by surprise.

"Even kill that bastard Kip," he threw in as he started the van and Caledonia burst out laughing, even though in the back of her mind, she knew he meant it.

Touching his sleeve, she smiled when he looked her way. "Thank you, Percy. You know I feel the same about you and Able."

His quiet nod reinforced his former statement and she knew the bond between her and the O'Reilly brothers would never be broken.

Caledonia watched her parents crawl into the car behind the van. Able sat at the wheel. She wished they would stay behind. If they got hurt in all this, she'd never forgive herself. Momma was stubborn and Poppa wanted nothing more than the chance to knock the shite out o' Kip. She sighed heavily. This time... This time she'd let him. Kip had stepped over the last imaginary line she'd drawn for him to cross.

The radio gave up-to-the-minute details on the horrific traffic jam. She said a silent prayer that no one was hurt too seriously and Kip was trapped in the long lines behind it. If nothing else it slowed his progress and maybe they'd get to the storage facility before him.

She leaned into the seat and propped her feet on the dashboard. It had been a long night and an even longer day so far. Eyes closed, she rested and sorted through the mass of jumbled thoughts. Several days ago, she'd made a major discovery. One she could never announce to the world of antiquity retrievals. It wouldn't boost her ranking in the salvage community. No. Struan wasn't a thing. He was a person.

His life was taken from him by a curse. Caledonia's heart sank, remembering the sadness in his face the moment he learned the truth. Disbelief warred with confusion as Mary's ghost explained his fate. Would he have believed Caledonia if she'd been the one who spoke those words? Maybe, maybe not. He trusted Mary. He knew Mary. The only thing he knew about her was her body and that they shared a love for the water.

Caledonia turned away from Percy and hoped he didn't catch a glimpse of the unwanted flush in her cheeks. A slow burn warmed her at the memory of their phenomenal sex and made her squirm in the seat. This was going to be a long ride. Squeezing her eyes tight, she forced the image of his incredible form, the taste of his mouth and the perfect fit of the two of them together to the recesses of her mind.

They had to save him.

Though she doubted Struan needed help. Kip was in for the surprise of his life when darkness came. A knowing smile upturned her lips. She felt positive Struan, armed with a Claymore and a *sgian dubh*, would win any battle that ensued. Unless, they had guns. Her chest tightened. Don't go there. She tried to calm herself. Kip abhorred violence. If anything, he'd hired a couple of poor slobs to help him move Struan in statue form. He definitely wouldn't do it himself. That required physical exertion and the possibility of getting dirty.

No. There wouldn't be violence. That wasn't his cowardly, thieving sort of way.

* * * * *

Panic tore through him. Something was wrong. He sensed motion yet could not tell if he was being moved or if his imagination played tricks. Non-functioning ears strained to hear but gathered naught. Maybe Caledonia was somehow moving him. Without physical functions, sight nor sound, Struan resolved to being held prisoner within this confine o' stone. If he was being relocated, Caledonia must've had a good reason. Determined to overcome the threatening torment of being locked away, unable to react, Caledonia filled his mind's eye, soothing the tension, relieving his angst.

Resurrecting her memory, he held her in his arms, tasted her lips and suckled from her breasts. *Caledonia.* His *fèilleil fiadh-cat.* Phantom nails scratched down his back. Her teeth teased his lower lip. *Och,* he knew his shaft ached to harden for her but lacked the ability to respond. Struan needed to be inside her, fill her over and over.

In his mind, he licked and kissed her flesh and laved her navel with sharp spikes of his tongue. A wicked moan rang inside his head. Her pelvis lifted. Her legs parted. A scent belonging to Caledonia and her alone tormented his memory. Dragging his tongue along every curve, he'd licked the salt of her skin but wanted more. The haven between her thighs creamed rich with her essence. He hungered for a taste.

Situating himself perfectly, he teased her lower lips with gentle nips and long, lavish licks, but refused himself the pleasure of ravishing her sanctuary. Instead, he took pleasure in tormenting her into another plane of desire. Tease her until she couldn't take any more then reap the rewards. Over and over, he kissed and nipped without separating her folds completely. She writhed and whimpered, begging him for more.

Moisture seeped from her crevice and he was lost, knowing she wept for him. Struan entered her with one long, deep swipe of his tongue. A flavor unlike any he'd ever tasted coated his tongue and rocketed his need skyward. This was Caledonia pure and uninhibited, giving him sustenance through pleasure. Though it lived only within his mind, Struan didn't doubt she'd ever fall below the level of this dream. Nay, she'd surpass it in reality.

* * * * *

Caledonia moaned aloud, waking herself. She froze, lost for the moment as to where she was or how she'd gotten there.

"That must have been some dream you was having," Percy teased.

Heat flushed her cheeks as she straightened her clothes and righted herself. It suddenly became apparent they were parked. "What happened? Where are we?"

"You fell asleep so I figured you needed it. If you look out the window into the side mirror, you'll see the storage facility across the street behind us." Percy nodded. "Able parked your parents over by that grocery store on the far end of the parking lot, so as not to draw attention when we both pulled in."

"How long have we been here?" Caledonia stretched.

"Just a few minutes."

Unusual heaviness lingered between her thighs and her panties felt slightly damp. Great, a wet dream. She'd had a wet dream in front of Percy. That was one he'd never let go and she knew it. Images of Struan flashed behind her eyes and made her smile inwardly. The dream felt so real. One time with him wasn't ever going to be enough for her. Not with the way this man dominated her mind even when she slept.

She caught a movement in the side mirror's reflection. A wimpy-looking man exited the storage locker she knew belonged to Kip. According to the records she had on him, he used it as one of his *antiquities exchange locations* as he called them. This gray building was one long, rectangular wall of storage cubicles, which lined the front, sides and along the back. A tall fence enclosed the building with a one-room security house at the gate. The paved lot around the building gave enough space for vehicles to park and maneuver to load and unload their goods for storage.

Today it appeared as if the security guard was nowhere in sight and the gate was left open. From the looks of the place, it was quite possible it lacked security in the first place.

"Able's doing a bit o' reconnaissance on the building," Percy stated as he watched the mirror on his side for movement.

"Do we know if Kip is inside?"

"We should when Able is done."

The suspense of not knowing was killing her as she stared into the side mirror, watching for anything. How long was Able going to take? Percy nudged her and she turned to see her parents walking along the sidewalk as if they were taking a Sunday stroll. Momma wore the broad-brimmed, red hat she used while gardening. Poppa stood at her side, keeping her between him and the storage facility. At the angle at which she had the hat tilted on her head, it helped keep his face shielded from direct view.

What were they thinking? She didn't want them getting hurt or tangled up in all this. Caledonia prayed for their safety. *Oh lord, keep those two out of harm's way. Please. I know they're a handful and strong-willed, but do your best.*

Able popped up from behind a garbage container, which sat two doors down from Kip's unit. The container sat in front of a space that had obviously been cleaned out at some point earlier in the day. He gave a slight nod with three fingers held up. He then walked out the gate, turned left and met her parents in front of the flower shop next door. Percy opened his door.

"It's clear. Kip is in there with two other men."

"How'd you know that?" Caledonia asked as she opened her door.

Grinning, Percy replied, "He held up three fingers, middle one included. That one's Kip."

Caledonia shook her head. Those two were incorrigible, as well as her parents. She and Percy hurried across the street. They met the others in front of the flower shop. A large cart of assorted flowers sat between them and the fenced lot. They had the perfect view of Kip's storage unit. It was number two-twenty on the front corner and was one of the more spacious. Corner storage units were big enough to back in a van and unload with the roll door closed. It also had another door for easier access.

"How are we going to get to Struan?" Momma asked as she pretended to shop for flowers.

"The way I see it," Percy stated, "we wait for the sun to drop, let nature take its course and during the confusion, we rush the place."

"I like that plan," Able chimed in. "As long as I get to hit someone."

"Again with the hitting," Caledonia said. Her brows bunched and she knew he noticed the confusion in her tone. Percy was normally the one who wanted to hit something. "What's gotten into you?"

"He just needs to get laid," Percy whispered loudly and laughed.

"Pent-up frustration makes a man crazy," Poppa added with a stern nod.

Great, just what she needed—a man with an overactive need to break something because he suffered from a case of blue-balls. Then again, she stopped as the idea sank in. It might be enough driving force for them to win if it came down to a fistfight.

She returned her attention to the storage unit. Nothing moved but the growing shadows along its front. The sky slowly darkened as the sun's last beams nodded off to sleep. Caledonia and her crew walked through the unguarded gate, leaving Momma at the flower shop to call the police if needed. The moment sunlight disappeared the fun started.

For a split second, her skin sizzled and the hairs on her arms and the back of her neck stood on end. Struan was awake. She knew it. Hell, she felt it in every living molecule of her body. Her heartbeat increased when she heard the crash echo from inside the storage unit. Something hit the opposite side of the roll-up door with a solid thud. If it were a cartoon, there would've been a shape molded in it from the force. Probably someone's face she figured. Poppa grabbed the other door's knob and found it unlocked.

On the count of three, Poppa jerked the door open. Percy and Able bounded inside followed by Poppa and Caledonia. The sight was nothing short of comical where Kip was concerned. He bobbed and weaved behind some big, brute of a guy who had squared off with Struan. Another rather large individual laid knocked out cold on the floor beside the roll-up door. In the back corner sat a pile of discarded junk. From the dirty look of the place, Caledonia was surprised Kip stood within its walls.

"Callie, what kind of a sordid trick is this?" Kip demanded, peeking out from behind the massive wall of what she could only assume was some sort of hired bodyguard. "What happened to the statue?"

"Magic, pure and simple." Caledonia practically purred with satisfaction that Kip failed once again to recognize the beauty of what occurred. His stupidity didn't matter. Struan's freedom did. "You wouldn't be in this predicament if you hadn't stolen from me in the first place."

"Stolen," he sputtered. "You're my wife. What's yours is mine."

"Divorced, Kip. D-I-V-O-R-C-E-D. Get that through your thick skull," she stated in a calm, deliberate manner from her position beside Struan. "Nothing I have is yours and that includes me. That's one thing you need to remember in that stupid pea-sized brain of yours."

"Caledonia." Struan's thick brogue and the way he said her name sent chills down her spine. She noted Struan spoke to her but never dropped his gaze from his opponent. "It is nice o' you to arrive but as you can see, there are games afoot. My *fèilleil fiadh-cat*, stand back and give me a moment to clear the room o' these arses, then you shall be safe."

The oversized thug lunged at Struan. Man on man, they fought. No weapons other than hand-to-hand. Struan's agility even with a heavy Claymore strapped to his back amazed Caledonia. His footwork matched that of any prizefighter. She watched in awe of his ability. The bad guy took a swing. Struan ducked and landed an uppercut to his jaw. The idiot swayed backward into Kip, who screamed and shoved the man back into the fight. With a shake of his head, he seemed to have cleared his noggin and stepped toward Struan again then stopped.

Struan remained still until the man swung first, throwing a right then a left. Both missed Struan's face by millimeters. His fists didn't miss their mark. Struan landed consecutive blows to the man's middle, causing him to grunt loudly and stumble. Not giving the man a chance to recover, Struan stepped and aimed for his head. A solid blow knocked him down for the count. He sank in slow motion to his knees then fell face-first to the floor.

"Cheap hired help," Kip yelled as he ran toward the door.

Poppa had other plans. He tackled Kip. The pair slid across the floor until the wall stopped their progress. Fin dragged Kip to his feet as he stood. With one hand balled in the front of Kip's shirt, Fin hauled back his other fist and before he could land the blow, the coward squealed like a girl.

"Not the face, not the face."

"Defend yourself like a man," Fin demanded. When Kip refused to do anything but quiver with his hands covering his face, Fin released him. "You ain't worth the effort. I don't understand what my daughter ever saw in you."

"This isn't the man I once loved, Poppa," Caledonia stated from directly behind him. "The Kip I knew got caught up in a lust for money that killed the kind, decent man I married." She stepped around her father and stared directly at Kip, who peeked at her from between his fingers. "Let this be your final warning. Don't cross me again. I walked away from everything I worked so hard to build and didn't fight you in court just to be rid of you. It won't happen again. Leave me be, Kip, or you won't like the consequences."

She leaned in close to his ear and whispered, "I have a copy of all your computer files. How else do you think I found you so easily? Push me and I'll destroy you."

Caledonia turned to walk away. In a move that surprised them all, Kip grabbed her braid, fisted it tight and jerked her backward. Before he got a good grip around her waist, Caledonia elbowed him in the ribs. Her poppa took a step forward and creamed him in the face with a meaty fist that broke his nose. Blood gushed. Kip cried out in pain, immediately releasing Caledonia and cupping his nose.

"I warned you," Fin claimed as he readied for another round. His brogue thickened with anger. "Never to lay a hand on my daughter. You didn't listen. Would you like another reminder?"

"You crazy old man," Kip yelled. "You broke my nose."

"Who you calling *old* man?" Fin raised his fist to strike again only to be stopped by Percy.

"I think he's had enough, Mr. Kavanagh." Percy glared at Kip and he shrank against the wall. "He ain't worth the time or energy."

"Aye," Fin replied as he relaxed. "You're right."

"Damn," Able muttered. "I didn't get to hit anyone."

Caledonia, Percy and Fin broke into laugher while Struan simply stared, looking a bit confused. Caledonia moved to his side and gathered his hand. The moment she touched him, her insides warmed. The heat in his gaze weakened her legs, making it difficult to stand steady. Damn, he was the perfect man.

"Where are we?" Struan asked. His fingers gently brushed her cheek.

"Edinburgh."

"South o' Loch Tay." He sighed with a sad shake of his head.

When he woke and realized he was no longer in the shed, he knew he needed more than to learn to dive. He needed the end to the curse. His *brathairs* were free. Mary's words he felt were truth on that matter. Then why not him?

How long must he suffer the constraints of the curse? How many times would he wake and not know where he was? This controversy clawed at his soul, opening a new wound to which he knew no salve to heal. He didn't like unanswered questions.

How had he gotten here? From the looks of it, he had been moved in stone form. He sensed Caledonia and her family was not the reason he'd been relocated, but they had somehow found him. Now they had faced danger because of him. This did not bode well with his sense of honor.

If he were ever to be able to offer Caledonia his heart, he wanted it to be whole. Not a partial night-only existence. When he saw her standing in the doorway while he made ready to fight, he made his decision. Find the end to the curse first then make peace with the ghost of his past. Turmoil brewed in his chest. The love of the dive battled with his sense of valor. He knew what must be done and refused to waver from his latest decision.

"Caledonia," he said, forcing his tone to sound convincing and not show the true disappointment he felt in his soul. He wanted to reach the bottom of the loch, but he wanted something else more. Looking at her, he knew just what that something was but he couldn't offer it to her. Not in his cursed state. He licked his lips and found the courage to continue. "It is time I return to Castle MacKinnon. I want to be free of this curse so nothing like this can happen again."

She knew the turmoil he must feel. He wanted to go home, but he also wanted to dive to the bottom of Loch Tay. She'd promised to help him do both. "Are you sure?"

When he nodded, she glanced across her shoulder at the others. "Anyone up for a road trip? If we leave now, we can swing by home, pack for overnight and drive Struan to Castle MacKinnon tonight. Dependent on traffic, we might even make it before sunrise."

"Nobody's going anywhere."

In sync, they turned to face a short man impeccably dressed in what looked to be a very expensive suit with high-dollar shoes to match. His distinctive features spoke of Asian descent. As did that of the three rather large men who surrounded him. They stood just inside the doorway. The tallest of the oversized goons stood behind him, staring directly at them over the shorter boss's head. The other two stood on either side and were just as intimidating in size.

Caledonia thought she recognized him, but try as she might she couldn't place a finger on who he was or where she'd seen him. His accent was undeniably from China, Japan or somewhere in that region, but she had no clue as to which fit his dialect. That wasn't her expertise. Protecting her friends and family, that was more her style. She stepped in front of everyone and stared directly at the thin, little man.

"Who are you and what do you want?" She did her best to sound authoritative. Standing to full height, chin tilted and shoulders straight, she stood at least a good couple of inches taller than her new opponent. He didn't have to answer. She guessed he was here to claim his prize. The statue Kip placed on the black-market auction site.

"My business is none of yours," he replied in a slow, smart-assed tone. Even though she stood taller than he, he somehow managed to still look down his nose at her, as if she were some sort of poor peasant and he was the king. He leaned slightly and looked around her at where Kip had run for cover behind the O'Reillys. "I've come for what is mine, Crosby. Where is it?"

The brothers looked at one another. With a nod, they separated. Able took a giant step to the left. Percy stepped right, leaving Kip out in the open. Still holding his nose with one hand, Kip's eyes widened with fear before he started to babble.

"Mi Tu Jang."

Mi Tu Jang, oh God, Kip didn't. Caledonia gritted her teeth and swallowed her gasp. She couldn't believe the idiot had gotten involved with this notorious art collector—thief described him better in her mind. Mi Tu Jang ruled the black-market art world. His ruthless reputation preceded him. Damn, this wasn't good. Her heartbeat increased and her palms sweated, but she refused to show fear. That would get them killed, if what she'd heard about this man was correct. He got what he wanted no matter the cost.

"Well, Crosby. I'm waiting. Where is it?" Jang repeated, not bothering to hide the growing irritation in his voice.

"I had it. Really I did. But it." Kip cut a glance at Struan before he pointed and stammered. "H-He stole it."

Mi Tu Jang's eyebrow arched as he stared Struan up and down. His face took on a comical twist. "You let this funny-dressed Scot steal from you? You really are pathetic. I want the money deposited into your off-shore account returned immediately."

In an unusual show of backbone, Kip replied, "I'm not doing that. It's not my fault. He stole it. If you want it, take it up with him. He has your statue."

"Is what he says truth?" Mi Tu Jang turned his attention to Struan.

"Aye." Struan's chest puffed and his voice deepened with an ominous edge that sent chills down Caledonia's spine. What the hell was he doing? Before she could speak, he added bitterly, "I have the statue. It does not belong to you."

"Ah." Jang nearly sighed his reply. "That is where you are wrong." He did a backward sidestep to his right, placing himself behind one of his bodyguards as he gave his command. "Retrieve what is mine so we can leave this dreadful place."

The three men shifted into combat stances, surrounding their boss. Percy looked at Able and smiled. Able thumbed his nose in an arrogant manner. The two brothers moved in unison, stepping around Caledonia. It didn't surprise her when Struan maneuvered to place himself directly in front of her and her poppa as a human shield.

"I got the one to the left, Percy you got the one to the right and Struan the middle's all yours." Caledonia didn't miss the humor in his voice. This was what he'd been waiting for, a good fight.

The other three men each took a step and pulled out handguns. Her heartbeat stalled and she couldn't breathe. Struan reacted faster than anyone she'd ever seen. The Claymore left its sheath in a blur. Metal clashed on metal. From right to left, the men's guns hit the floor without a shot being fired. This pissed off the biggest guy in the middle. He turned, ripped a loose rusty pipe from the wall and spun it like a weapon as he closed the distance between him and Struan. Caledonia tried to intervene, but Poppa grabbed her around the waist and dragged her away from the fight.

Able and Percy both held their fists at the ready. Percy nodded at Able without taking his eyes off his opponent. "You think these two read their fortune cookies this morning?"

"Nah," Able retorted, calmly. "If'n they did, they would've known they were in for an arse-kicking."

The man in front of Able lunged, performing some sort of overblown martial arts maneuver. Able sidestepped him and landed a solid left to his cheek. Percy had similar luck with his opponent. He sidled up beside Able as they both readied for the second attack. "You think they watched too many of those Kung Fu action movies?"

Able replied by moving his lips without making a sound then said, "I believe you're right, my brother."

"I'll take barroom brawling anytime over martial arts bullshit," Percy claimed as he dove headfirst into his opponent's forward advance. Able followed suit. The O'Reillys' fighting skills were well renowned in the world of Scotland's barroom brawlers. Usually, Able wasn't the one who hungered to fight, but he never walked away once one started. Caledonia worried more about Struan. She bit her lip as she studied his every move.

Struan's opponent was armed with a long, metal pipe. From the look on his face, it didn't bother Struan. He rolled that heavy Claymore's hilt around in his hand as if it were featherlight. Facing one another, they circled, each sizing the other up and searching for a weakness. Whereas Struan appeared aloft and prepared, the oversized goon seemed tense and ruled by anger. He acted first, swinging the pole at Struan's head. He ducked and before the bad guy regained his balance from the overzealous movement, Struan tackled him.

The pole went flying across the room and rolled to a stop at Mi Tu Jang's feet. He simply looked at it with a bored stare. Caledonia didn't like his overly calm demeanor. Though his outward appearance showed a lack of concern, she sensed he plotted his next move. She stepped back, keeping her father to her right and Jang in front of her and a little off to the left. At no time did she intend to let that man out of her sight.

A wild scream echoed. Loud grunts and groans and the sound of fists to flesh repeated in the air. Glass scattered as one of the men's head hit the rear van door window. She flinched yet still managed to keep Jang in her peripheral vision. The action-packed scene between her men and Jang's made her heart pump faster. Able took a roundhouse kick to his midriff and went flying backward against the wall. Percy had blood dripping from his lip, but it didn't seem to faze him.

A movement near the door caught her eye. The two men Kip hired were sneaking out, escaping the chaos. Caledonia snorted. If Kip could reach the door, he'd run too. She had no doubt of that, but he was trapped between the corner, the pile of junk and the battle *royale* that took place.

Able rebounded and took down his man. Was that a smile on his face? Oh lord, he was smiling. Her head shook. He really did need to get laid if a fight brought him happiness. Percy clocked his guy with a solid right hook and the man finally sank to his knees, eyes rolled back and he was out.

Struan. Where was Struan? Caledonia panicked. She'd taken her eyes off him for a second and now he… A body slid over the hood of the van and landed near Kip in the corner. Kip squealed and inched away from the unconscious man. Struan rounded the front of the van, picked up his sword where he must've dropped it and walked toward her. The fight was over.

She heard the scrape of metal and spun to see Mi Tu Jang flick the pole into the air with his foot and catch it in his hand. An unreadable haunted gaze filled his eyes. He spun the long metal pole in his hand like a master dojo instructor. When he moved, his steps were precise, as were his actions. The hired muscle had nothing on this man. It became obvious to her, every article she'd ever read and rumor she'd ever heard about him held an ominous truth.

Within a matter of seconds, his lightning-fast skill swiped the feet from under both Able and Percy. Claymore in hand, Struan measured his opponent. She sensed more than saw Poppa move to assist. She couldn't let him or anyone else for that matter get hurt. This ended now. The men had their fighting fun. Now, it was time for a woman to step in and handle the matter.

Staying out of Jang's line of sight, she grabbed a folded, metal chair from the pile of discarded junk. In a move that would've made the finest of television wrestlers proud, she pounded him in the back of the head with every ounce of strength she could muster. He spun to face her. Caledonia clutched the chair, readying for another swing. Mi Tu Jang took one step then fell face-first to the floor. Her jaw dropped. She'd knocked him out.

"That's my girl," Fin cooed as he walked over and took the dented chair from her. "You okay?"

Caledonia simply nodded, still not believing she'd hit someone hard enough to knock them out. Yet, the proof lay at her feet, breathing but not moving. Warm hands clasped her elbow and she forced her gaze to lift. Struan's eyes were lit with humor. Did he find what she did funny? Thinking back it really was sort of comical the way she'd brought down a renowned criminal. Struan's smile touched her heart and her lips twitched into a thin smile. He was safe. She threw herself into his welcoming arms. The gentle stroke of his hand down her back eased her shock.

"You did a fine job, lassie," he whispered, pressing his lips to the top of her head in a light kiss. "You sure you're all right?"

"Aye," she said, pushing back and tilting her head to see his face. "We just need to get out of here." She shot a questioning gaze across her shoulder to the others. "Anyone still game to help me get Struan home tonight?"

"Aye," the O'Reillys stated in unison.

"I think that'd be nice, dear," Aileen's voice turned their attention to the open doorway. She stood holding a wrapped bunch of flowers in her hand. "We should leave right now. As I purchased these, the florist heard the commotion over here and dialed the authorities."

Kip tried to make a break for the door, but Struan halted his progress. Arm held straight, Claymore pointed at his throat, Struan challenged Kip. "You nay be going anywhere, Kip. You must pay for all the wrong you've done to Caledonia. Fight me like a man."

Kip fainted. Percy, Able and Poppa looked at Struan's surprised face and shrugged. Without a word, each of them stepped over him and headed for the door. Caledonia squeezed Struan's hand. She stood on tiptoes and kissed his cheek.

"That meant more to me than you know. Thank you. We've got to go now. Hurry. I'll explain everything in the van."

He didn't question her, simply followed as she and the others darted out the gate and across to the shopping center's parking lot. No one hesitated. Able and the Kavanaghs walked quickly to their car in as casual a manner as possible so as not to bring suspicion, got in and drove away. Percy slid into the driver's seat of the van. Since there was only room for one passenger up front, Caledonia chose to sit in the rear of the van with Struan. They jumped in through the side door of the blue panel van, slammed it shut then she pounded on the wall behind Percy's head as a signal they were in.

Sirens cut the air and her chest tightened. Would Kip try to have her arrested? The van rolled backward as Percy maneuvered from the parking space. Through the rear door windows, Caledonia saw flashing lights. She scooted on her knees closer to get a better look. Two police cars rolled into the fenced lot and came to a stop behind the vehicles outside Kip's open door. The lights in both parking lots lit the action for all to see. A crowd grew.

Percy drove across the shopping center parking lot to the farthest exit away from the storage facility. The farther they got, the less she saw but she knew she'd seen enough.

Too bad for Kip. She snorted, letting a smile upturn her lips. This time he lost.

Chapter Eleven

Caledonia turned and met pure surprise mixed with fear. Struan squatted in the front corner. Both hands were palms flat against the inside walls of the van, doing his best to steady himself. What was wrong with him? Then it struck her, for a moment she'd forgotten his situation.

"What form o' witchery is this? We ride in the b-belly o' a beast," Struan sputtered as his gaze darted from side to side as if searching for the closest escape route.

She crawled over to Struan and sat back on her heels. Gathering his face in her hands, she made him look at her.

"It's okay, Struan. You're riding in the back of the van we told you about. This is how we'll get you home. It runs with a motor. It's like a horse-drawn carriage without the horse."

She placed a gentle kiss upon his lips. "I promise, nothing will happen to you."

One hand at a time dropped from the walls and around her waist, tugging her close. She felt his distress ease as he kissed her forehead, her cheeks then lowered to her lips. Gently he massaged her back. Fingers trailed upward at a slow, sensual pace, kneading every muscle until he cupped the back of her neck with one hand while the other fisted her braid.

"Caledonia, seems you have saved me again."

Though he knew not how he'd awakened in Edinburgh, he knew where he was now. In the arms of the woman whose image kept him sane while imprisoned. His memory did not do her beauty justice. Each intake of air filled his senses with her scent, a faint hint of roses. Caledonia soothed the growing despair of all that confused him in this new world.

Desire warmed his soul and guided his kiss into a passionate war of tongues. Neither relinquished power to the other, which made him smile inwardly. She gave in her kiss as well as took what she wanted. Her hunger for him could not be mistaken and he didn't intend to let her down.

No, his *fiadh-cat* deserved everything he had to offer in the ways of pleasuring a woman. Struan stroked her hair. The braid teased his palm with its thickness until he reached the end and worked the band off that held it. He hugged her tight, kissing her, while both hands untangled her braid. Umm, how he liked the sensation of her silky strands as he ran his fingers through its length. Never had a woman's hair fascinated him like Caledonia's. He broke from their kiss as he lifted her hair to his nose and inhaled. Roses and a subtle hint of honey—light, airy and fresh.

Struan couldn't get enough. He gathered her hair in both hands and drew it across her shoulders to frame her face. With it still gently wrapped within his fingers, he cupped her face and smiled. Though very little light entered the van, there was enough for him to see her and she him. Tenderly, he traced her lower lip with his thumb while holding her gaze.

"No words match your beauty, my *fiadh-cat*." Desire controlled his tongue, making him sound low and husky. Her lips parted slightly as if she readied to speak but he stilled her voice with a finger to her lips. Gliding his finger from her lips to her chin, he guided her face at an angle, which better suited his mission.

Please Caledonia.

The list of questions he'd acquired during his entombment could wait. For now, he had a woman in need of pleasure and that came first. He lowered to her neck and nibbled ever so lightly. The hissed intake of air through her lips let him know she liked it so he continued.

Gentle nips to her flesh along her neck to her collarbone garnered him the perfect reaction. A low moan rose from deep in her throat. When she reached for his kilt, Struan caught her by the wrists and stopped her advance.

"Nay, my *fiadh-cat*." He kissed her palms then met her lust-filled gaze. "For now, your pleasure is my pleasure. I want you to keep your hands here." He guided her arms to her sides. "And not move them. Can you comply with my wishes or do I need to tie them?"

A visible shiver hinted she liked the idea and a bolt of pure need shot straight to his bawls. Yet indecision skittered through her eyes. He cupped her chin and waited patiently for her response. Seconds ticked until a simple nod gave him permission to proceed. At last a sexually adventurous woman. He sighed happily.

Struan lifted the hair from her ear and leaned in close, placing his lips near its sensitive flesh. Intentionally, he released a long breath of warm air and enjoyed the subtle mewing sound she made. A great sexual adventure was all about the tease, the foreplay. He traced her lobe without actually touching the tip of his tongue to its rim. Her eyes closed and she leaned into him.

A quick nip to her lobe produced a sultry gasp, letting him know she liked the game he played. Her body reacted well. Light-as-a-feather strokes of his palm from her neck to the curve of her breasts had her nipples standing at full attention and he hadn't even touched either of them. Struan's mouth watered to suckle the tender mounds but she wasn't quite ready. Not yet.

"Caledonia," he whispered, letting the heat of his breath warm her exposed ear. His hand captured her breast and held it gently as his thumb circled the nipple. Even through her clothes, he felt it harden. "I want to see the beauty o' your breasts, to taste them, until I've had my fill."

When she lifted her shirt to her head, he stopped her. Caledonia's arms were wrapped within it. Her head was covered as she halted mid-removal.

"Let me help you," he stated. His voice deepened. Caledonia's breasts perched in a lacy garment he couldn't resist. He eased the shirt off then helped guide her into a more relaxed position, elbows bent, hands behind her head "I like the way this position lifts your breasts, making them sit perfectly as if waiting for me. Please don't move and let me do the touching."

He massaged each breast through the lacy garment. Gently at first, then he increased the pressure until she moaned. Good, she liked it harder. Struan tugged the lace down under her breasts. The sight of her perky breasts, nipples pointed, surrounded by the feminine lace made his shaft twitch. She was his to take. Struan closed his eyes and refrained from rushing to seek his own pleasure. When he'd calmed his need he continued.

Struan sucked one nipple in deep while kneading the other breast, alternating between soft and hard pressure. Her breathing increased and she wiggled slightly as if trying to close the gap between them. He smiled around her nipple then flicked it with his tongue right before he grasped it with his teeth and tugged, gently. Caledonia gasped and shivered in ecstasy, fueling him onward. He moved to the other breast and quickly nipped the tender bud, blew on it then tugged it deep into his mouth.

"Yes," she moaned in a guttural tone, letting him know she enjoyed the roughness. Needing more, he slipped off her shoes and socks. Remembering her earlier actions, he unbuttoned her trews, pulled the metal contraption down with a zip and helped her out of the manly garment along with another lacy item, which covered her treasure. He lifted it to his nose and noted it was damp with her delicious essence.

Hard and hungry for her, he dug deep for the strength not to sheath himself in her heat. Not yet, he whispered mentally. Please Caledonia then receive your own release along with her second or third. He smiled. When she attempted to reach for him, he commanded she stop and hold still. This time the pleasure was all about her needs, not his. It surprised him that she listened.

Struan spread her legs with gentle strokes of his hands up and down the insides of her calves, knees and thighs. Each time he came close to touching her shaven mound, she bucked and sighed. He lowered to lie between her thighs and gathered her buttocks in his hands. The perfect banquet sat opened for him to feast. At this he would not fail.

Slow, long swipes along the inside of her thighs made her cry out, "Please."

He smiled as he lifted to look up her body to her lust-darkened eyes. "Please what?"

"I need," she gasped, inhaled then continued on a stuttered breath. "I need you, Struan. Please help me."

"Aye, my *fiadh-cat*." Struan sampled her slit with a deep flick of his tongue. She bucked, trying to rush his efforts. He would not be hurried.

He delved into her sheath with the tip of his tongue, tasting all that was Caledonia. Over and over, slow mixed with quick as he licked, suckled and drank from her healthy fountain of desire. Struan could've lingered within her folds forever but her pleas stilled his movements. Had he heard her correctly?

"Straun, please, please fuck me. I can't take it. Please fuck me," she begged.

Instantly, his bawls contracted and his shaft strained heavy with need to be inside Caledonia. Resistance failed. He battled the urgency rushing through his veins, lifted from his feast and blazed a path of kisses and nips up her body.

"Say it again, Caledonia," he breathed against her lips as he hovered a hairsbreadth apart. "Tell me what you want."

She gathered his face in her hands and stared directly into his eyes. "Fuck me, Struan. Fuck me hard. I need you."

The barrier of resistance snapped. He plunged deep within her in a solid stroke as he captured Caledonia's mouth in a roughly passionate kiss. She lifted her hips, pumping into his, matching his rhythm, fast and furious, harder and harder. Though he knew she'd be bruised from the forceful pounding, he couldn't stop. Neither would she let him. If he slowed, she dug her heels into his rear, demanding he increase the pace.

Caledonia's nails scratched down his back and he sensed she would've drawn blood if not for his tunic. His kilt bunched around his waist didn't hamper his ability. Yet he was thankful he'd removed his Claymore upon entering the van. That on his back would've been a tad uncomfortable as he pleasured his wild cat, especially when she somehow managed to flip him onto his back without breaking their connection.

Like in his dream, her hair curtained them. It tickled his nose as she rode him. He grasped her hips as she ground into him repeatedly. Struan grappled for control. His beautiful wildcat rode him into oblivion. The sight of her breasts bouncing as she arched while rotating her hips tore at his restraint. He couldn't take it anymore. Struan sat upright, seating her fully. He clasped onto one of her breasts and tugged at her nipple. She screamed his name as her sheath clenched his shaft.

Finally, he'd pleasured his *fiadh-cat*. Struan lost himself in their mutual release. His seed pumped into her, mixing with the cream of her orgasm. He maneuvered them so he could lean against the wall with her cradled in his arms.

He kissed her brow then rested his head against the wall, eyes closed, as he whispered, "My *fèilleil fiadh-cat*, you have ruined me for any other."

Ruined him.

Hell, she didn't think she'd walk again, much less have sex comparable to this with anyone else ever. Too weak to move, Caledonia snuggled closer, breathing in his earthy, masculine smell. A combination of underwater scents mixed with Struan's essence, which appealed to her basic needs in life. Family and diving.

Headlights from the traffic behind them gave limited light, but it was enough for them. With her cheek pressed to his chest, she realized she was the only one of the two completely undressed. Her eyes widened, taking in the sight of his tunic. His kilt was raised, leaving him, technically, still clothed. Weakly, she sat upright. He'd teased her breasts unmercifully, eating her until she came, and made love to her, in a rough and wild bout of hot sex. He turned her on beyond belief.

No orgasm in her short sexual history ever shattered her system like this one. Though he'd refused to let her touch him while he'd teased and tasted her, he'd quickly eased her concern with his touch, soft words and gained her trust. He'd driven her to the edge of ecstasy with his foreplay, and then brought her home with a solid fast and furious fuck. Every ounce of her shivered. Ripples of contentment shimmied through her.

Caledonia searched his face. Masculine and at peace with his eyes closed, he looked the portrait of innocence. She knew he wasn't or at least thought he wasn't, especially with the way he'd fucked her. He definitely fell into the category of an experienced man in that department. She bit back the smile that threatened her lips.

What else did she know of him? Very little other than what Mary told her. Caledonia touched her watch and lit the dial. They had at least another hour before home. Now was as good a time as any to talk. Reluctantly, she reached for her shirt without leaving his lap. Struan's arm circled her waist and stilled her movements.

"Something wrong, my *fiadh-cat*?"

She returned her gaze to his face. A questioning concern filled his eyes and warmed her heart. "Nay, Struan. I think it's best if I get dressed in case we stop. I don't think Percy would be delighted to catch us having sex in the back of the van."

Even though he probably heard them. The thought brought a flush to her cheeks, making her grateful for the dim light. If she were lucky, Percy wouldn't say anything even though in her gut, she knew he knew. The radio volume increased when she screamed Struan's name earlier in her heated moment of passion. Oh God, she hoped he wouldn't tease her about this.

"Percy is no concern," Struan replied, handing her shirt to her. "It is the anger o' your father which would bother me. Percy I can handle, but your father has a mean right hook." He shot her a wink that made her laugh.

"That he does," Caledonia managed to say as she adjusted her bra and slipped into her shirt. The jeans were another issue. It meant getting off his lap and losing the comfort and connection of him nestled inside. Though he was no longer hard, she was still aware of his size and placement. He didn't deflate to nothing immediately. Nope, he remained a decent girth and length, enough so he didn't just slip out once they were done. She bet if they wanted they could stay connected, snuggled together as they slept in each other's arms. Unfortunately, that was a theory she'd have to wait to test.

On a heavy sigh, she lifted from his lap and gathered her panties and jeans. Out of the corner of her eye, she saw him right his clothing. Once dressed, Caledonia's conscience sprang into play as she sat beside him. This was awkward. What did she say? How did she say it? Again, she'd managed to fuck him without any thought or inhibition. She leaned back into the wall. He must think she was some major sort of whore, especially after she'd followed his sexual instructions without hesitation.

He gathered her hand in his and soothed the tension she felt blooming in her chest. How did he do that with simply a touch? Caledonia stared at their hands. His deep brogue caressed her ears as he spoke.

"Who is this Kip? Is he your husband as he claimed?"

Was there a hint of jealousy in his words? A smile teased her lips but she managed to suppress it. "No. Not anymore. Kip and I were married. It didn't work out so we got divorced."

"He was a fool to let you go," Struan stated as if it were a worldwide fact. Caledonia had difficulty swallowing past the lump that swelled in her throat. His fingers caught her chin and turned her to look at him. "You are the most beautiful being I have ever met."

"Thank you," she replied weakly. His thumb absently caressed her lower lip as if it were the natural thing for him to do. His darkened gaze seemed mesmerized by his thumb's actions as he spoke.

"You claimed this Kip stole from you. What did he steal and do you want me to get it back?"

"He did steal from me. After tonight, I doubt he'll do it again." She had difficulty thinking straight with his thumb teasing her lip as she answered, "Besides, I already have what he took."

For a moment, he seemed to be mulling over the information before he asked his next question. "How did I come to be in Edinburgh? Last I remember, I watched the sway o' your gorgeous bottom as you walked out o' the shed right before the curse took me. The next, I woke in a strange place surrounded by a couple o' thugs."

He'd watched her arse. Oh Lord, Caledonia couldn't breathe. That was the largest part of her and he'd been watching it jiggle as she walked. His fingers changed position, sliding along her cheek and into her hair as he turned to face her. There was nowhere she could focus but his face. Flickering light from the headlights behind them gave his eyes a sensual darkness.

"You've got a fine arse, my little wildcat. And I like it." He kissed her lips. Not passionately, not intended to light another fire of desire, but caringly yet not lacking heat either. Caledonia relished his taste, the gentle tease of the tip of his tongue, which glided across her lower lip as if sampling her every flavor.

Breathing him in deep, Caledonia gathered the courage to ask him something that nagged at the back of her thoughts. "Struan, I'm sorry the curse is not over. The words I spoke to free you is only half a freedom and I can't imagine how painful that is to tolerate."

Struan sat back. Absently his fingers stroked through her hair as he stated, "This is not a fault caused by you, Caledonia. Don't be thinking you caused any o' this pain o' which I suffer from this curse. If not for you, I would never have experienced the pleasure o' the dive."

Caledonia slid closer to him and took his hand in hers. All the way to her soul she wished her touch eased his angst as his had done for her. "Hopefully, when we get you back to Castle MacKinnon, one of your brothers might know the answer." She bit her lip against the words but failed to halt them as they tumbled through anyway. "Then maybe, once you're freed, you can continue your dive training."

Silence fell between them for several long minutes. She knew this was hard on him. This being torn between doing something he loved like diving and this desperate need to be rid of the curse. Which she understood. Hell, if it were her, she'd probably have collapsed from the weight of the confusion.

She cut a sideways glance his way as something else popped into her head. What did he feel when he returned to stone? Could he hear her talk to him? Could he see? *When he returned to stone.* That sounded awful. Before she stopped her mouth, words fell out she prayed didn't seem too nosey.

"Does it hurt when you change back into statue form? Do you see or hear anything? What do you remember?"

Struan lifted her hand and kissed her knuckles before he answered, "I remember your arse." He stroked her nose playfully with the tip of his finger, which made her smile and roll her eyes at the same time.

"That's it. Nothing else." She sensed his hesitation. It seemed as if he chose his words.

Struan's voice lowered, sadness laced his tone. "Heat controlled my spirit and burned my soul, then I could not move. I could not see nor hear. I felt trapped within my flesh, until an angel filled my mind and guided me to inner peace." He touched her cheek and smiled. "You were my guardian angel. Now tell me, how did I get to Edinburgh?"

"Oh," Caledonia sighed, loving his poetic words at the same time realizing she never answered his question. "Kip stole you, put you in his van and drove you to Edinburgh. He sold you on an antiquities black-market website and planned to exchange you for the money at the storage bin, where we found you."

His brows bunched and she knew he processed the information and prepared another round of questions. His eyes widened as he realized something.

"I'm what Kip stole."

"Aye, handsome. That you are," Caledonia teased. "I just wish I could've seen his face the moment you shifted from stone to man. That must've been a jaw-dropper for him."

"He was not pleased to see me when he opened the doors," Struan stated. His chest puffed and a hint of humor laced his tone. "I woke in a place I did not know. You were not there. He opened the doors. I had my sword drawn ready to attack. The one you called Kip ran and hid behind one o' the other men."

Caledonia snorted. "Sounds like Kip the coward all right."

Struan nodded and continued. "The first guy jumped me from behind so I slung him as far as I could. He hit the wall, headfirst and did not move again. You know the rest. That's when you rushed to my rescue."

"It wasn't much of a rescue," Caledonia said. "You had it under control when we got there."

"Aye, but I would not have known where to go when I left. Without you, I would have been lost." He turned and kissed her lips. Pure heat shot straight from her lips to the tips of her toes. Damn, did they curl? It sure felt as if they did.

They separated and it took all she could do to concentrate on anything other than jumping his bones again. She cleared her throat and focused on learning more about the man other than the size of his cock and his awesome ability to kiss.

"Tell me about your home and your brothers."

She sensed his pride the moment he spoke. "My *brathairs* and I are close. My sister, Akira, is the only female o' the brood. If what Mary said be truth, two o' my older *brathairs* are free. Gavin and Ian."

"Is Akira the baby?"

"Nay, the twins, Donnell and Dour, are the youngest. Their mother was my father's second wife, Siusan." Struan leaned closer to her and added with a laugh as if a memory tickled his brain, "Now those two were a handful. Not a day went by they did not get into some sort o' trouble."

"How so?" She liked hearing him talk about his family.

"Ever the practical jokesters," he stated point blank. "I remember a time when we were on a hunt. While Dour kept Ian's attention, Donnell switched his prize arrows with sticks. Mind you, Ian's a bit particular about his arrows. He hones them each to perfection. The moment a deer crossed Ian's path, he loaded his bow, only to miss."

He started to laugh uncontrollably for a few moments, which infectiously made her laugh as well. He wiped his eyes as he gathered his composure. "Speed o' the angels beneath their feet saved them from Ian's wrath. It took me and Gavin hours to calm him enough not to kill those two."

"It sounds like a fun family," Caledonia said.

"It was." Struan's tone sobered yet hinted of anger. "Until it was stolen from me, from us."

Caledonia thought carefully for a moment before she spoke. Pain rippled thickly off him. "I have no words to give back what was lost. But I can take you home and hopefully with the members who are there, you can rebuild and move forward. Start a new life. This may not be what you imagined your life to be, but think of it as a new challenge."

She licked her lips, then added. "I promise to help in any way I can to find your missing family members."

He pulled her into his lap and held her close. She heard his deep inhale and felt him nuzzle his face into her hair as he claimed, "I believe you, Caledonia. There is a reason you have been sent to watch over me and I am thankful to the heavens for you."

Leaning into him, she relaxed. His words washed over her, cutting a path directly to her core. How had this man managed in so few hours to burrow his way to the center of her heart and commandeer her undivided attention?

Great sex, fancy words and kisses that scorched her brainwaves, that's how. She sighed contentedly.

Chapter Twelve

It was after midnight before they finally left Loch Tay for Castle MacKinnon. When Percy and Able returned home for a change of clothes, they found their older-model Land Rover had been repaired by their mechanic friend and left at their house. It provided more room for the ride than their mother's compact car and more comfort than the van.

The Kavanaghs stayed behind. Aileen packed a basket of food and drinks for the trip. Percy drove. Able sat in the front passenger seat as navigator. It took some convincing to get Struan back into another vehicle. He was certain they were some sort of magical beast and wanted nothing to do with them.

It took Fin lifting the hood and giving him a quick lesson on how it worked to gain Struan's trust in the *magical beast*, as he called it. Thinking of how patient her father had been with Struan kept a thin smile on her face. Struan was an apt student and if anyone had worthy knowledge to share, it was her father. He'd kept that old van of theirs working for long past its natural years. To her, Fin Kavanagh was one of the smartest, most honorable, loving men she knew.

Her brows pursed. Maybe that's why things didn't work with Kip. He just didn't measure up to her father. But Struan. He was a man built from an entirely different mold. One that resembled her father's in so many ways—he'd shown honor, pride and love of family. She swallowed the sigh that threatened to escape as she watched Struan, who stared out the window into the darkness.

Since they'd left the house, he'd sat quiet and non-moving to the point he almost resembled his statue state. Did he still fear the magical beast? Caledonia reached for his hand, which seemed glued to the seat as if he held onto it for life. When he looked her way, she did the best she could to relieve his anxiety.

"I understand," she said in as light a tone as she could muster. She wanted to ease his distress and make him smile. "I don't like riding with Percy driving either."

"Hey," Percy snapped. "If you like, I can pull over and let Able take the wheel."

"Oh no," Caledonia retorted kiddingly. "That would be even worse. Bad enough, he's the one reading the map."

"You know, Percy," Able replied. "We could just toss her out right here and make this a men-only trip." He turned to Struan. "When you lived in Lochsbury, were the women good looking?"

"Aye, the women o' Lochsbury each held a beauty o' their own." From the look on his face, she could tell he was processing their conversation before he continued. "I do not understand this driving, but it seems to me Percy is in fine command o' this magical beast."

Percy grunted in agreement. Able laughed and Caledonia smiled.

"I was just kidding to get your attention. Percy is a fine driver. You sat there quiet for the past hour and seemed so tense. I thought it might be the ride."

"Nay." Struan shook his head. His thumb absently caressed hers. "I was thinking o' my *brathairs*, my family and time lost."

He turned away and stared out the window again. Silence returned but this time, her hand remained in his. The slow methodical rhythm of his thumb drawing circles on the back of her hand kept her tuned into him. His breathing. His heartbeat. The heat from his hulking size filling the backseat. Suddenly, it seemed as if it were only her and him alone in the vehicle.

Caledonia closed the gap between them. The connection of their hands remained unbroken. She shifted her little finger and matched his strokes in his palm. For each circle he placed on the back of her hand, she imitated it in his palm. No other touch needed to be made for her blood to warm. She rested her head against the backseat and closed her eyes. Images of what she wished they could be doing danced inside her head.

Naked. Flesh upon flesh. His mouth teasing her nipples, and though it wasn't actually happening, they pearled inside her bra anyway. She wished the vision were real. Caledonia swallowed hard against the solid lump in her throat. Her breath hitched when he lifted her hand and the warm moisture of his kiss sizzled her skin. Need hummed within her, causing her to shift in her seat.

Struan released her hand, laid his arm across her shoulder and tugged her snug against him. He tilted her chin with his fingers as his lips found hers. For a split second she panicked, remembering Percy and Able sat in front. His kiss ended as quickly as it started as they shifted to her ear. The heat of his words tickled and sent a ripple of desire across her flesh in the form of tiny chill bumps.

"If'n we were alone." He directed her hand to his lap, letting the solid rod beneath his kilt finish his thought for him. She didn't need him to speak for her to understand. He wanted her as badly as she wanted him.

Caledonia glanced at the two in the front then back to Struan. Leaning close to his ear, she whispered, "I wish that too."

Palm open, she smoothed his kilt, making sure to linger on one particular hard wrinkle the most. Though she watched Able and Percy, she caressed Struan's cock. She rested her head on his shoulder while continuing to gently glide her hand along the center of his lap. After several minutes, he captured her wrist. His graveled whisper made her smile.

"My *fiadh-cat*, you have the touch o' an angel." He lifted her hand, delicately kissed each fingertip then kissed her palm. "I prefer to enjoy my pleasure inside o' you and not in my kilt."

Even though it was dark in the backseat, she couldn't miss the passionate look in his eyes. A promise lay within their depths she wanted desperately to claim in the near future. Her insides growled with a hunger only he could satisfy. If Percy and Able weren't in the vehicle, she'd straddle his lap and ride this Scottish God into oblivion. That's how hot he'd made her with nothing more than a few strategically placed sensual kisses and seductive wording. Damn. She breathed deep, taking in as much of his masculine scent as possible.

Her mouth watered as he lowered to her lips. Anticipation knotted in her chest. She wanted his taste, his touch and the sensation of his flesh upon hers. Caledonia's heart pounded and her breathing stopped for a split second at their initial contact. Percy cleared his throat and Caledonia jumped, breaking them apart. She met Percy's amused stare in the rearview mirror and she shot him an I-can't-believe-you-did-that glare. A quick cut of her eyes sideways and she noted Able concentrated on the map. She knew from his posture he'd caught them kissing as well.

"If we got the directions right," Percy stated as his gaze left the rearview, "Castle MacKinnon should be coming into view around this next bend."

She felt Struan stiffen. He craned his neck as if trying to see around the curve in the road. Caledonia followed his direction. In slow motion, a lighted castle came into sight. It appeared miniature in size, situated among the rolling hills and trees of the countryside. As they traversed the road, its tremendous size became more obvious. Five tall towers stood proud as the castle's sturdy protectors. One on each corner with the tallest stationed in the middle.

Percy made the turn onto the long lane that led to the castle. Struan sat on the edge of his seat. Anticipation and excitement wafted off him in waves, which made her smile. He reminded her of a child on Christmas morning the moment they saw the presents from Santa. At the end of the lane, Percy entered the large, circular drive and pulled to a halt in front of the stairway that led to the main double doors.

Struan fumbled with the door handle so Caledonia reached across him and assisted with opening it. He slid out, stood frozen for a moment then, as if it were a common action, he held out his hand for her to take. He helped her to her feet then smiled at her.

"Thank you for bringing me home, Caledonia."

Before she had a chance to respond, he sprinted for the stairs, dragging her along with him. She worked double time to keep up. Where he took them two at a time, she ran full pace from step to step and somehow managed not to stumble or trip. Caledonia nearly slammed into him when he came to a dead stop at the top of the regal stone staircase. The bright light over the doorway illuminated a pair of mahogany doors. She gasped for air to compensate for her exertion as she admired the hand-carved set.

A phenomenally detailed scene of a large man with a sword drawn in battle stance filled the main section of each. She didn't get the chance to enjoy the artwork before he forcefully shoved one of the doors open. It amazed her it wasn't locked. Either there was no crime in the area or they were the most trusting individuals on earth to leave the front door unlocked.

Something whispered in the air around him. *Welcome home.*

Letting go of her hand, Struan stepped inside. His heart raced. His senses filled with the essence of home. Familiar scents rushed his being and wrapped his soul in a warm glow. Home. Home. Eyes closed, he soaked it all in, letting the comforts of this place wash over him and rid his every fiber of unwarranted distress. Home. Home. He breathed deep.

He took a step and tripped over a strange bag in the hallway. It took several steps to right his balance and keep from falling, but not before he knocked a flower-filled vase from a small table beside the door. It shattered, scattering flowers and water everywhere. The crash echoed loudly, rolling from the entranceway and down the long main hallway.

He didn't care. Struan caught sight of something he desperately needed to see. He hurried to a huge tapestry, which hung midway down the hall. He didn't hear the footsteps coming from the room off the hallway behind him. Every ounce of him was tuned in to the family portrait on the wall. Trembling fingers reached to trace his family members but were halted by a hand that came down hard and strong on his shoulder.

Fighting skills engaged. Before he thought better of it, he grabbed the wrist, jammed an elbow into his attacker's ribs then twisted and flipped the man over his shoulder. The oversized hulk of a man landed on his back at Struan's feet with a solid thud. In a flash, Struan had his *sgian dubh* in hand and at the man's throat before he realized his mistake. A deep voice he thought he'd never hear again rumbled from the doorway of the room behind him.

"Struan, is that anyway to greet Ian after all these years?" Gavin's brogue lightened his soul as a laugh rumbled from his oldest *brathair*.

Instantly, he released his hold on Ian as his *brathair* brushed his long hair out of his face. "Ian," Struan gasped as he tugged him to his feet and clasped him in a bear hug. "Forgive me. It has been a long journey home and I—"

Ian cut him off. "No need to explain, Struan. I understand. I followed that road as well."

Gavin grabbed Struan into a hug the moment he released Ian. "You are a fine sight for these old eyes, my *brathair*."

"As are you." Struan's voice cracked as he choked back the tears. Grown men did not cry. For several long seconds, he feared releasing Gavin would cause him to wake and realize he wasn't home, that it was only a dream.

"It is okay to release me now, Struan. You are home to stay." Gavin's deep timbre gave him the strength to stand straight and let go from the hug. When Gavin nodded toward the front door, Struan remembered he hadn't arrived alone. "Who are your guests?"

Struan turned to find Caledonia stood in the front doorway with Percy and Able. He strolled over to her and gathered her hand. "Welcome to my home, Caledonia. I want you to meet my *brathairs*." He didn't look anywhere but her beautiful eyes as he added, "Percy and Able, I owe much to you both for my safe return."

He kissed her knuckles then turned to face his *brathairs*. "These are two o' my *brathairs*, Gavin and Ian." Each nodded when he said their name. He released her hand and lowered his to the small of her back as he guided her forward.

"This is the lovely Caledonia Kavanagh o' Loch Tay," he stated in a regal tone as he presented her to his *brathairs*. "I owe my life to her. She found me at the bottom o' Loch Tay." He held her hand to his heart as he lingered, lost in those cerulean blues. She looked even more inviting standing within the walls of Castle MacKinnon.

The clearing of a throat jarred him from the mystical hold Caledonia's being in his home placed upon his soul. He quickly announced his other two newfound friends. "And with us are the O'Reilly *brathairs*, Percy and Able, o' Loch Tay as well."

"It's nice to meet you," Caledonia replied. Her voice seemed unusually low and weak as if she were intimidated—or overwhelmed. "Struan has spoken fondly of both of you and of his home."

Struan searched her face for any signs of feminine distress. He'd heard of women fainting if they became overexerted, though he doubted Caledonia fit that category. She'd shown him nothing less than pure, strong will and cast-iron inner strength. Traits he found admirable in her. She reminded him of his sister. When she didn't meet his gaze, he knew something bothered her.

"Hi, I'm Izzy," an adorable woman with odd hair stated in a friendly tone as she stepped into the hallway. It looked as if her hair had been extremely short at one time and had bright-white tips that covered half its length. Struan couldn't help but stare at the anomaly. Izzy noticed his dismayed look and quickly explained as she ran a hand through her strange hair design. "I used to keep my hair cut very short and dyed it white, but Ian asked me to grow it long for him and let it return to its natural shade."

When Ian locked his hand possessively in Izzy's, Struan was astonished. The self-proclaimed bachelor found a woman. He was grateful Caledonia interceded on his behalf as she replied, "It looks fine. Struan's not acclimated to this century yet. Please excuse him for staring." Her gentle elbow poke in his ribs reminded him of his manners.

"I apologize, milady." He bowed respectfully then looked at Ian. "I did not mean to impose ill upon your woman, Ian," he stated sincerely and hoped they forgave him. If he wanted to stay home, he knew better than to insult one o' his *brathairs'* ladies. He truly hadn't meant to, it just happened. Her hair was the oddest in nature he had ever seen.

"Apology accepted, Struan," Ian announced with a slanted smile on his lips. He leaned toward Struan and whispered, "There's much to be said o' a woman with odd hair, my *brathair*. She has a fiery spirit unlike any I have ever known, nor will I be able to tame her completely."

Izzy playfully nudged Ian. "We've had this discussion many times. I'm not an object to be tamed nor owned."

"Aye, my *dona leannan*." Ian kissed the top of her head as he laid his arm across her shoulders. "That we have."

Struan was dumbfounded by Ian's display toward this woman. It wasn't his nature. Ian had his heart broken and vowed never to settle upon one woman again. If he heard Ian right, he called this woman named Izzy, his *dona leannan*, his naughty lover. A hand upon his shoulder brought his attention to his *brathair*, Gavin.

"I would not have believed it either, my *brathair*," Gavin stated. "Izzy has her hands full."

"As do I."

The sound of another woman's voice came from the doorway of the room off the hallway where they had been gathered prior to Struan's entrance. Gavin moved to her side and wrapped an arm around her waist. His face filled with love as he looked upon the woman then returned his attention to Struan.

"Struan, this is Ericka, my wife."

Instantly, Struan knelt at her feet. Head bowed, he stated, "I pledge my life to the safety o' my *brathair's* wife and the new lady o' Castle MacKinnon."

Ericka gathered his head in her hands and urged him to his feet. "Struan, it's not like that in this era. We *all* live here as a family. No one rules the other. Each of us is free to make our own decisions and come and go as we please. We work together for a common goal. To find and free every missing MacKinnon brother."

When she hugged him, Struan looked to Gavin. His hearty laugh eased a smidgeon of the confusion that rattled Struan's thoughts. He breathed in deep and accepted the sisterly love Ericka offered. He glanced from one to the other. One brathair married. The other in love and probably headed down the same path. Struan couldn't help but reach for Caledonia the moment Ericka released him.

Was *he* headed down the road to matrimony? He tried to shrug off the thought. Now was not the time for such fancy. There were *brathairs* to be found. Except, the thought lingered and took root. Gavin and Ian found *gaol*, love. Why not him? Struan met Caledonia's gaze and read uncertainty. Something truly bothered his *fiadh-cat* and it didn't sit well that he would have to wait to find out what.

"Come," Ericka said as she turned toward the room she came out of. "Let's sit and hear the tale of how you were freed."

As the others followed, Struan waited while holding Caledonia's hand, keeping her at his side. He tucked his finger under her chin and gently lifted. When she didn't meet his gaze, he knew his fears were right. "What is it that has you worried, my *fiadh-cat*?"

"Nothing." Her feigned smile didn't fool him.

Caledonia didn't give him a chance to ask anything else. She was still mentally kicking herself in the ass for not thinking past the task of bringing him home. She tugged from his grip and entered the room behind the others. This night had taken a turn toward a world of uncertainty for her.

What did she think would happen?

That was just it. She hadn't thought. No. She'd simply acted on impulse, which normally wasn't like her. He'd never promised her more than pure pleasure, which he'd accomplished. Struan gave her the best sexual experiences of her lifetime. Was that what she would miss? She cut a glance his way and knew it wasn't the reason her heart hurt. She'd miss the man.

Her insides swirled and gurgled with a combination of excitement for Struan because he was home and selfish regret because he was home. She hated herself for the latter. She held no claim to him. What they'd shared was sex and nothing more. She tried desperately to convince herself as she forced her legs to carry her into the room. Wasn't the real concern in helping Struan escape the curse completely? She'd vowed to help him in any way possible. For some stupid reason, her heart had gotten involved and twisted her line of thought.

Come morning, while he rested in stone, she, Percy and Able would return to their home at Loch Tay. She could research curses from there. Would she ever see him again? Her heart turned to lead and sank in her chest, struggling to maintain a steady beat. It disturbed her to think she'd miss him as much as her heart hinted. How had this happened? How had she fallen for Struan in such a short time?

Determined to help him the best way possible, she pushed her personal desires aside and made the conscious decision to keep her hands to herself and let Struan decide his fate. Struan belonged at Castle MacKinnon with his family. He needed time to adjust to his new life. *A life quite possibly without her in it.* That thought made her stomach curl into a pit of mixed emotions. Struan's life was his to live. Not hers to guide, even though she'd found him and set him free. Nor was he a possession to own like an artifact she'd retrieved from the watery underworld.

He wasn't truly free, now was he? His image in stone speared her brain and tore at her soul. No, he lived half a life. There had to be some way she could help him and save her heart from the possibility of losing him in the process. His friendship would be better than nothing. Caledonia plastered on a smile and took the seat on the couch offered to her by Ericka.

Glancing from person to person, she saw so many similarities between the brothers that she could've guessed they were Struan's siblings without being told. Gavin stood taller than Ian, but Ian had broader shoulders and seemed to be overall heavier in muscle. From the fit of the jeans Ian wore, his thighs were massive. Caledonia shot her gaze upward to study their faces. Gavin's eyes were a dark shade of green. Ian's were blue. Both kept their long, dark hair in ponytails, which hung to about mid-back.

The two women in the room were as different as night and day. Ericka wore thin-framed reading glasses perched on top of her head. Her shoulder-length auburn hair was pulled away from her face and held by a silver clip at the base of her neck. Izzy's hair was in mid-transition and all over the place, but still looked stylish on the tomboyish woman. Where Ericka seemed more demure and refined, she got the impression Izzy was outgoing and a bit more flamboyant, if she read Izzy right. Green eyes were the only trait the two had in common. Except for the hair. Caledonia guessed when Izzy's returned to its natural color, it would probably be a shade of red.

Struan lagged behind and it wasn't until he walked in holding a bunch of battered flowers they remembered the crash.

"I tripped when I came in and broke a vase," he muttered sheepishly. "Where would you like these?"

"That's my fault," Izzy said. "In a rush to go to the bathroom, I dropped my bag there when we got home. I meant to move it to the pile with the others by the stairs, but didn't get the chance to before you arrived. I'll take those." Izzy reached for the flowers. "And I'll clean up the mess so don't you worry about it. Come sit down for now. It will keep. We want to hear the tale of how you were rescued." Izzy's eyes widened as she spun to face Caledonia. "How'd you know the anti-curse? Where'd you get it? It's not exactly common knowledge."

"I can explain." The hauntingly lyrical brogue of Akira whispered around the room as she slowly appeared.

"Akira," Struan gasped. "You are spirit just as Mary claimed."

"Aye," Akira replied, floating to a stop in front of him. "I taught Mary the anti-curse and in turn she taught it to Caledonia."

"Why did you not come to me as Mary did?"

"The angels granted me the right to protect my *brathairs* until their release from the curse. My spirit is confined to the grounds o' Castle MacKinnon. Only once have I been removed from my home and that was through the use o' black magic." She shot a smile to Gavin and Ericka. "If not for the love o' Gavin and Ericka, I would still be trapped within a magical cell by a descendent o' Hume MacGillivray."

"A MacGillivray." The words seethed angrily from Struan's lips and pure hatred shown in his eyes. Caledonia knew that name belonged to the man who'd placed the curse on the MacKinnons.

"Aye," Gavin stated, settling on the arm of the couch beside Ericka. "We have a living enemy. He seeks our *brathairs* and the book o' black magic that Hume used on us."

"We've got to rid this world o' him," Struan growled. Waves of anger washed over Caledonia and his pain seemed to be her pain. She swallowed hard and sat on her hands to prevent touching him.

Ian moved beside Struan and laid a comforting hand on his shoulder. "We have tried, my *brathair*. MacGillivray controls a form o' black magic o' his own. It is how he has escaped us."

Struan sat on the arm of the couch next to her. His body heat warmed her to her toes and she had difficulty suppressing the urge to reach for him. She didn't like the anger flowing from him. She wanted to ease his pain, to hold him, but resisted.

"If you can't leave here, how did you contact Mary?" Caledonia asked, trying to redirect the conversation from this MacGillivray in hopes Struan's anger would dissipate.

"She came to me." Akira motioned to Struan. "We have a common bond. That thread led her to me and in turn she found you. The woman who would free Struan from his prison."

"He's not exactly free." Caledonia met Struan's gaze. The sadness in those deep-sea blues chipped at the wall she tried desperately to build around her heart. Why was he sad? He was home. That's what he wanted. "He turns to stone with the rise of the sun."

Caledonia dragged her gaze from Struan to Akira. The knowing arch in Akira's brow and the slim smile teased Caledonia's curiosity, but it was the specter's words that confused her most.

"Oh, I'm sure that will change." She seemed to pause dramatically as she shot a look from Ericka to Izzy that ignited Caledonia's suspicion. "In time."

"Do you know how to break the curse?" Caledonia couldn't hide the sudden anticipation in her voice. Was there really a cure? If so, why didn't they share it?

Ericka took Caledonia's hand in hers. "There is a way to break the curse, but it isn't something we can do. It's something that can only be experienced for the spell to break completely."

"What is the answer to my remedy?" Struan demanded.

Gavin smiled then stated point blank, "The answer lies within you. Not one o' us can tell you the path to follow. It's one you must choose for yourself."

"Trust us," Ian interjected. "Sleep on it and I bet the light o' truth shall lead you to freedom." He nodded slightly toward Caledonia, which confused the hell out of her.

Why were they speaking in riddles? Why didn't they come right out and say what needed to be done? Anger slithered up her spine but before she reacted, Struan took her hand in his and kissed her knuckles. The sadness no longer lingered in his eyes.

Had he understood what they meant? Would he tell her so she wasn't left in the dark? She glanced to see Percy and Able were grinning as if they knew a secret. How did they figure it out and she missed it? Caledonia started to ask but swallowed the words. Nothing came to mind that sounded even remotely nice so she decided to let it rest and think it through. Maybe she'd figure it out for herself.

Chapter Thirteen

They sat for hours talking and sharing stories. Gavin, Ericka, Izzy and Ian's recent adventure ended differently than Struan's tale of discovery and release. Though there was happiness and joy over Struan being home, there also was a tinge of sadness over the dead-end trail to another brother. Gavin, Ian, Ericka and Izzy had just returned to the castle about half an hour before they arrived. The group had gone on an expedition into the Grampian Mountains in search of an abandoned church, where Izzy had seen a picture of a statue online. It wasn't a brother. It turned out to be some patron saint of some blessed charity.

That failure didn't overshadow Struan's return. The brothers talked as if time hadn't separated them for centuries. Caledonia couldn't help but smile at the way Percy and Able made themselves at home. The O'Reillys fit right in, drinking and helping Struan expand on the fight that occurred in Edinburgh when they'd found him.

Caledonia learned how Ericka came to Scotland because of her Aunt May. It was a funny story where an American afraid of travel suffered the trip to save her eccentric aunt from real estate fraud and found love in the process. She wished she had the opportunity to meet this Aunt May. From what Akira, Ericka and Izzy claimed, this woman had spunk. She found an old diary in a box of books she bought at a bookstore in London. The words of love and family dedication drove her to locate and buy Castle MacKinnon, where she quickly became enamored with the ghost of Akira, who had written the diary May had found.

To hear Izzy say it, Aunt May was the real reason any of the brothers were free. If May hadn't believed, no one would've tested the words in Akira's diary and learned the truth of what happened to Clan MacKinnon of Lochsbury. In the wee hours of the morning, Ericka suggested they turn in and continue their discussion at breakfast. Izzy and Ian showed the O'Reillys to their guest rooms.

Gavin tucked Ericka into the crook of his arm then nodded to Struan. "Your bedchamber is better than you left it. I think you will like the soft mattress, fine linen and fluffy down comforter. The pillows are soft as well. Would be a grand place to sleep if'n sleep is your plan." Gavin waggled his eyebrows as he led Ericka out of the room and toward the staircase.

Struan laughed and Caledonia struggled not to blush. Had he just implied she sleep with Struan? Before she could correct the mistake, they were gone and Struan turned to face her.

"I have been waiting all night to ask you again what is bothering you, my *fiadh-cat*." He clasped her waist with both hands as if it were small in size. She swallowed. He did make her feel tiny and petite. "Don't be telling me nothing. I sense you have a heavy heart."

Looking into his eyes, how could she admit the selfish feelings coasting through her soul? She wanted him with her. Caledonia licked her lips, but before she managed to construct the right words, his mouth brushed over hers. Gentle touches coaxed her to respond. How could she resist the persistent pressure from his tasty tongue?

Tender tongue massages whisked her insecurities to the back of her mind. If all they had was here and now then so be it. Caledonia leaned into him and let his warmth fuel her need. A soft sigh escaped when Struan lifted his lips from hers. His darkened gaze contained a promise of pleasure she was too weak to deny.

"Come. Let me show you to my chambers."

He took her hand and she followed. At the far end of the hall, he turned left and walked for what seemed an eternity to her. Every few feet, he stopped and pointed out something of importance, from a tapestry, to a painting, to an object from his time that hung upon the wall. His excitement became her excitement. The love for his home and family was genuine. At the bottom of a staircase in the back left corner of the castle, he turned to her. It took a second for her to gain her bearings and realize they stood at the entrance to one of the four corner towers.

"This leads to my bedchambers. I wish to take you there and share intimacies with you, Caledonia." Struan's brogue deepened with desire and made her shiver with a hunger for this man that came straight from her core. Just being in his presence, listening to him speak of things close to his heart, had her hot and horny for the ancient Scotsman.

She couldn't speak. No words formed so she simply nodded her consent. Struan swept her into his arms and carried her upstairs. At the top, Caledonia turned the knob and Struan pushed open the door with his foot. The room was lit by the soft glow of strategically placed candles. They entered into the sitting room of Struan's bedchambers. A large couch sat in front of a fireplace with a beautiful marble mantle above it. Hardwood covered the floor for as far as she could see.

Struan slowly released her, letting her slide down the length of his body, until her feet touched ground. Every inch that skimmed him as she stood brushed against the healthy hard-on she felt beneath his kilt. He led her to the room off to the right of the fireplace.

The door was open and candles had also been lit in there, giving the room a romantic glow. Caledonia had her suspicions as to who was behind it but didn't understand the why. A huge bed sat in the center of the room. A window was on either side of the bed and beneath those were a pair of nightstands. The bed had been turned down and made ready for them. Rose petals were scattered on the floor and across the pillows. A few even coated the sheets.

Designed to entice romance if ever she saw it. Caledonia couldn't help but smile at all the trouble Ericka or Izzy or both had gone through for them. Thinking back, Izzy had disappeared under the presumption she went to clean up the broken vase and water. She'd been gone a rather long time. This was where Izzy obviously disappeared to.

"Come, Caledonia, we haven't much night left." He lifted her hand to his lips. The heat of his breath across her knuckles as he spoke undid any last strands of resistance that may have lingered in her conscience. "When darkness befalls me at sunrise." He cupped her face in his hand and held her stare. "I want your beauty to be the last I see until I wake."

Her insides melted. There was no denying how she felt about Struan. She bit her lip, halting the words of her heart from escaping in a deluge of rampant emotions. Struan needed time with his family. What he didn't need was a girlfriend. Girlfriend. Lover. Whatever. Caledonia gave herself a good mental shake. He needed the chance to adjust to this life before he'd ever be ready for a relationship. She still couldn't help how she felt. Deep down she knew she'd fallen ass over teakettle for Struan MacKinnon.

She led him to the side of the bed then turned to face him. After placing a tender kiss to his hand, she released it and began the art of stripping slowly for her man. Though she doubted they had a future past this moment, she wanted this last hour to be a memory that would last a lifetime.

Struan's heartbeat quickened as he watched her sensual movements. Deft fingers lifted the shirt over her head while her hips swayed to a silent melody. *Och*, she was beautiful. He reached for her. Caledonia had other ideas. Her head shook as she guided him to sit on the bed. The light kisses she placed in his palms heated his blood. She draped his arms over her shoulders then undid the lacy garment that held those magnificent breasts captive.

That was an item of clothing he wished he could be, a protector of Caledonia's breasts, secretly holding them, caressing them throughout the day, hidden beneath her outer garments. Ummm… He sighed at the fanciful image. Only she could make him want to be a bra—at least that's what he thought she'd called it if his memory was correct. At the moment, she had his brain fogged with lust. Struan smiled, watching his little wildcat tease him senseless.

With the clasp undone, the sexy, slow glide of the bra straps down one arm and then the other, while her hand held the material to her breasts, made him lick his lips. Her breasts were almost free for him to taste. She stepped between his thighs, slightly closing the gap between them. He massaged her shoulders, urging her closer but she resisted. Caledonia held the bra in both hands and shimmied it across his face. The wonderful scent of roses filled his nose. The smell of Caledonia was forever emblazoned in his brain and would always remind him of her.

He reached for her breasts but she halted his advances, grasped his wrists and returned his arms to drape across her shoulders. The smile wiped from his face the moment she took those full round globes into her hands. His mouth dried and his lips parted, stunned by the show. Caledonia lifted, massaged and fondled them in a way he desperately wanted to do. When she tweaked her nipples, tugging them into perfect pearls, his shaft stood at attention.

"*Och*, Caledonia, you be killing me," he gasped on a graveled breath.

"Nay," she replied. A wicked smile touched her lips and the look she gave him set his soul on fire with need. "I promise not to kill you, but I guarantee you'll be dead tired when I'm done with you."

The flesh of his thighs burned from her touch as she dropped her hands to his knees and slid them upward beneath his kilt. She came close but didn't touch his solid length. The trail of her fingers along his inner thighs, from knee to near his shaft and bawls, over and over, had him aching like a young buck in heat. The dance of her tongue across her lower lip made him swallow hard against the urge to capture her mouth and take charge of this devastating game of lust she played. It took every ounce of control not to act upon his growing need.

His heart stopped for a split second when she sank to her knees and disappeared beneath his kilt. Never had a mouth felt as good as Caledonia's. He fisted the sheets in exquisite agony the moment her delicate tongue licked him from bawls to the thick tip. The flick of her tongue around the head then in its tiny slit nearly sent him over the edge. Moist heat coated him as she took him into her mouth. Not fully, but enough to please and tease him into oblivion if he didn't stop her soon.

"Caledonia," he gasped. Her head popped up from under his kilt. The sexiest smile he'd ever seen split those hot lips.

"You like?" she asked playfully.

"Aye," he replied on a heavy breath. "I like too much." He placed his fingers under her chin, bent over and kissed her. "I want to be inside o' you, my *fiadh-cat*. Let me feel you gloved around me."

Struan lifted Caledonia to her feet and wasted no time removing the remainder of her clothing and undoing her braid. He gathered her in his arms then turned and gently laid her on the bed. The only time his eyes left hers was when he removed his tunic over his head. His kilt pooled around his boots as he stepped out of them and climbed onto the bed. Her sensual tease and touch had him ready, but he wanted her in the same heightened state of desire as he.

Starting at her bare feet, he nibbled and kissed his way to heaven. The sweet taste of her flesh watered his mouth and increased his hunger for a sample of her essence. He nuzzled the soft lips of her feminine sheath then gathered her flavor in a deep, long lick. Caledonia's moan thrilled him to the core and made his cock twitch. He tickled and suckled her clit until she trembled in orgasm, giving him the nectar he loved to taste upon his tongue. Though he could drink from her forever, time played against them.

He crawled the length of her body, kissing and tasting her flesh, inch by inch. If the curse did not threaten to take him soon, he'd spend every hour possible pleasing Caledonia. Hovering at her entrance, Struan held his weight on his legs and forearms. His fingers tangled in her hair. The feel of her legs around his waist, poising him for admittance into her heat made his heart swell. She was the most beautiful woman to ever cross his path.

"Caledonia," he whispered, studying her eyes and soaking in the passion he saw there. "I am blessed by your presence in my life, my *fiadh-cat*." He entered her in one solid stroke then pulled back, leaving only the head inside her warmth. It tested his resolve to hover in this position, when all he wanted was to pleasure his woman and hear her scream his name.

His woman? Just the thought had him teetering on the edge of release. Struan dug deep to hold on as the reality of those words settled in his brain. Aye, Caledonia was his woman, he decided. He knew who and what he wanted and hoped she felt the same. Struan plunged into her, seating himself as deep as possible. *Och*, her heat soothed his angst and readied the words from his soul to pass his lips.

"Caledonia, my *fiadh-cat*," he claimed as he held her gaze with his. He had to see if her desires followed his. He wanted her. He needed her. "You have cast a spell upon me that I do not wish to break. I want you to help me find the end to this curse."

Tears slipped from the corners of her eyes and panic tore through his chest. Did she not feel the same? Had he rushed this by speaking frankly on how he felt? He cared deeply for her. He didn't want to lose Caledonia. He hoped the tight sensation in his chest was the makings o' love.

"I did not mean to upset you. I do not want to lose you, Caledonia," Struan whispered as he tried not to choke on the knot that bound around his heart and sat at the base of his throat. As he started to pull back, her legs tightened, preventing his retreat.

"Struan, I..." She didn't speak any more, simply cupped his face in her hands and tugged him into the hottest kiss of his life.

Her desire washed over him, sending his heart into overtime. Time played against them, this he knew as fact. Minutes ticked to seconds before sunrise. He needed her to know how much he wanted her before the curse played its evil game. Struan pumped into her fast and furiously as their mouths plundered each other in a war of tongues. Her nails raked down his spine, leaving a trail of marks that branded him as hers, which thrilled him to his soul. Caledonia was truly his wildcat lover and his alone.

The moment her heels dug into the back of his thighs, he knew she was close to reaching her pleasure. He broke from their kiss and gathered her face in his hands.

"Open those beautiful eyes, Caledonia. I want to share in the joy o' our love and see it in your eyes." She responded with a wide-eyed, hot stare that sent a jolt of molten heat through his system straight to his bawls. Pure love shone in those eyes making him want for nothing more than to please his *fiadh-cat*, now and forever.

She met him thrust for passionate thrust. Heavy breaths fell in sync with one another as their pace increased in a mad dash for shared orgasmic ecstasy. Sooner than he liked, his name caressed his ears as her sheath contracted, soaking him in her juices. Lost to her love, Struan's shaky grip on his control disintegrated, stripped from him in the most pleasurable way, saddled deep inside his woman, his love. Caledonia milked him o' his seed, filled his heart with love and wrapped him in a cocoon of blissful peace within his soul.

Out of the corner of his eye, the first rays of morning sun poked their unwanted tendrils through the curtain's edge. Panic overwhelmed him as he hurriedly rolled off Caledonia. He knew as stone he'd crush her. Severe pain cramped his heart, ceasing its function. Fire laced every breath in his battle to intake air. Extreme heat singed every ounce of flesh, setting his system into a furious pace to cool him. Sweat soaked him but did not ease the warmth within his veins or across his skin. Biting his lip, he suffered in silence, taking with him the beautiful image of Caledonia in the throes of passion.

This eased his angst and soothed his soul. She was his reason to wake come evening. She was his reason to live. Struan relaxed, eyes closed as he awaited the fate of the dreaded curse to claim his being for yet another day.

His thoughts went into overtime as his body froze. He had an idea of what saved his *brathairs*, but did not realize the extent with which it occurred. He ticked off what he knew. Both *brathairs* had been awakened from the curse by a woman. So had he. Both *brathairs* appeared to be in love. He suspected the women they loved had something to do with their escape from the curse.

But what?

Struan struggled to think it through. The heat of Caledonia's body reached him through the thick wall of stone between them. Knowing she rested at his side gave him peace. His thoughts would not rest. Over and over he played the different scenarios inside his head as to what led to permanent freedom. Nothing came.

Exhaustion threatened his brainwaves as something finally dawned. His *brathairs* were in love. Did *gaol* lay the final card in this deadly curse's game? Struan would've laughed if he could've. That had to be the answer. For nothing else would have saved his *brathair* Ian.

Come evening, he knew what he needed to do. Now all he had to do was pray she felt the same.

* * * * *

The whole trip home, Caledonia couldn't wipe the long faces of Struan's family from her mind. Though they'd asked her to stay, she knew in her heart it was best for Struan if she left and let him rebuild his life. In time maybe they'd cross paths again. Maybe without her—an outsider— they would share the cure for the curse with him.

It still peeved her knowing they knew how to break it but wouldn't come right out and say it. They kept talking in some sort of cryptic codes that she construed as Struan had to find the answer on his own. *Some family.* She snorted as they pulled into her driveway at home.

Dead tired, she made her way into the kitchen. The O'Reillys followed her. Her parents sat at the table.

"Well?" Aileen asked.

"He's home," Caledonia replied as she plopped into the chair beside her momma and accepted the teacup.

Poppa slid the morning paper to her. "Seems Kip got what he deserved. He's been arrested. According to the article, he's been under investigation for a while for illegal art dealing. Being caught with the black-market kingpin only cemented the allegations."

"Oh," Percy chimed in as he leaned against the counter. "With all the excitement that's been going on, I forgot to tell you. Kip's bankrupt. Big Mike told me and Able all about how Kip ran the business into the ground. He heard everything's going up for auction next month."

Caledonia shrugged. "Doesn't matter. We don't have the funds to buy any of it."

She stood and without saying a word went upstairs to bed. Halfway up the stairs, Streak bounded ahead of her. When she entered her room, he sat proud as he could be on her pillow. A half smile upturned her lips as she scooted onto the bed next to him and snuggled him close.

God, please keep Struan safe. Help him find his way. She issued the silent prayer as exhaustion seeped through her system. Not only had her night been a whirlwind event of crime fighting, a road trip to Castle MacKinnon, and an early morning of phenomenal sex, but also she lost the perfect man.

Images of Struan sporadically flashed in her dreams, tormenting her soul. This was for the best. He needed his family and the answer to the curse. Not a woman. Not a *fiadh-cat*. The memory of his pet name for her sent a sliver of warmth to her soul.

She loved him. No matter what she tried to tell herself, she'd fallen in love with the ancient Scotsman. A tear slid down her cheek and Streak's rough tongue did it's best to wipe it clean. His tender effort made her smile.

"I love Struan," she whispered against Streak's fur.

* * * * *

Several days came and went. It didn't matter what she was doing or where she was. Each time night fell, she knew he woke when her skin sizzled and the tiny hairs on the back of her neck and arms stood on end. Damn. She rubbed her arms as she sat on the end of the dock with her feet dangling in the water. How long would it take before these sensations stopped? And why were they happening to her?

Absently, Caledonia slipped the stone Struan gave her from her pocket. She thumbed circles on the smooth side, cradling the rough side in her palm. It was an odd little rock that was strangely vibrant with a multitude of colors when held in the sunlight. Maybe that's why he selected it from the bottom and gave it to her. He saw something special in it she'd missed. Funny. She let a thin smile tug at her lips. One night underwater and Struan plucked a natural wonder from its mists. Though it held no monetary value, it was priceless to Caledonia. Struan had given it to her. She returned it to its safe place in her pocket.

Streak scurried to her, rubbed against her side and meowed until she lifted him onto her lap. He wasn't content to sit still until she persistently scratched behind his ears. "Little bugger," she whispered. "Not happy unless you've got all the attention."

His soft meow she took as a yes and laughed.

Heavy footfalls landed on the dock behind her. Caledonia stood, cradled Streak against her chest and turned. Her breath stilled on a gasp in her lungs. Struan walked toward her at a gait that seemed to take forever. It reminded her of those exaggerated slow-motion scenes in movies, as if time stood still with her vision on nothing but him. She hated to admit it, but he was all she wanted to see.

When he reached her, he smiled and her heart did a flip. Caledonia swallowed her excitement and prayed she didn't show it in her voice too much when she asked, "What are you doing here? You need time with your family."

"Nay, Caledonia," he said. His low timbre tickled her ears with the voice she thought she'd never hear again. "I have been a stubborn fool. What I need is time with you."

Oh God, he didn't just say that. Her insides nearly burst with joy but still she struggled to remain calm. "Your missing brothers…"

"His missing brothers can wait," Gavin stated from behind Struan.

Struan turned so she could see Gavin and Ian stood several feet behind him on the dock. When she looked at him, she knew he read the question in her eyes without her saying it. "It seems I am not the most pleasant o' men to be around at the moment."

"That is an understatement," Ian retorted with a hearty laugh.

Struan leaned in close and whispered, "Think you and I could find a quiet place to talk?"

Caledonia nodded toward the boat as she released the kitten. "How about out on the loch?"

"Milady, I would be eternally grateful for a few moments o' peace out on the water," he said as he gave her a mock curtsy.

"If you'll excuse us, gentlemen," Caledonia said as she walked over to the boat and climbed aboard followed by Struan.

"By all means, milady," Gavin replied. Without being asked, he and Ian helped un-tether the boat.

The moment the boat made its way from the dock, Aileen Kavanagh rounded the shed from her hiding place and stood beside the two brothers. "You think this will work?" she asked.

"By the will o' God, I hope so," Gavin stated.

"Aye," Ian seconded. "I pray this works. The only peace we get with him is during the day."

"You are bad," Aileen scolded teasingly. "Come to the house. You boys must be hungry. I made a nice meal. Fin and the O'Reillys shall return soon from the pub and we would love for you to join us. Besides…" She nodded toward the loch. "It looks like we are in for a long night."

"Milady, you may be right on that one." Gavin replied as he and Ian followed her to the house.

* * * * *

Something inside guided Caledonia to a special spot on the loch. Neither had spoken a word until they weighed anchor. She turned from securing the boat and landed in Struan's arms.

"Caledonia, I've missed you," he stated breathlessly. "When I woke and you were not there, my heart sank. I made the decision you were better off without me and tried to let you be. As you can see, my *brathairs* think me to be an ornery beast without you. While I slept in stone, they brought me here so when I woke, you would be near. They gave me no choice but to see you and ask the question weighing heavily on my soul." Sadness shone in his eyes. "Why did you leave?"

Her throat tightened. Being in his arms heated her blood and stirred her desires. The confused, questioning gaze in his eyes tore at her decision. She licked her lips then answered honestly, "I thought I would be in the way. Your family seemed to know the answer to the curse but didn't want to tell you. I thought if I wasn't there, they'd share."

Struan laughed heartily, holding her close. Though his laughter added to her confusion, his scent permeated her senses and stirred her hunger for the man. Umm, she'd missed him. She allowed only a few seconds of delight in his arms before she pushed back and glared at him.

"What's so funny? They weren't exactly being forthcoming with the anti-curse. They kept talking in riddles."

He leaned his forehead to hers and stared directly in her eyes. "The answer is right before our eyes, Caledonia. It just took me being without you to understand my suspicions about the cure were right."

"I don't understand," she replied on a hushed breath. The closeness toyed with her decision-making skills. All she could think about was stripping him.

Struan released her and straightened. "After tonight." He wagged his eyebrows at her as he spoke. "You will. What say we go for a swim?"

He didn't wait for her answer. He stripped right in front of her. Naked and proud he dove over the side. Caledonia couldn't believe she was doing this. Automatically, she looked around, making sure no other boat was near. Night had fallen. The loch was quiet and most with any sense were docked. Lifting her eyes to the full moon, she prayed no one noticed them. She quickly stripped and followed him over the side.

Cold chilled her to the bone but it didn't last. Struan was suddenly wrapped around her the moment she broke the surface. What surprised her even more, the cold held no effect on him. His cock pressed rigid between them as he held her close. Together they moved as one to remain buoyant beside the boat without separating.

"I have wanted nothing more than to hold you in my arms, Caledonia, and make love to you," Struan said. His passion-filled gaze warmed her to the core. The coldness of the water was forgotten as his words coated her skin with a heated promise she'd never forget. "I have dreamt o' being inside o' you, here in the loch, in the place where you saved me. This is the spot where you lifted me from my grave, is it not?"

Caledonia couldn't speak. She simply nodded and that was good enough of an answer for him.

His lips found hers. She couldn't wait. She wanted him. Lip upon lip, tongue on tongue, she returned his kiss. Every second of the days she missed him were relayed through that mouth–on–mouth touch. The cold around her dissipated as she shifted, hugging his waist with her legs. Struan grabbed the anchor chain with one hand for leverage and it was all they needed.

In a swift upward push, he entered her. Caledonia groaned against his lips. This was heaven. Never had she made love in the water. With Struan, it seemed like the most natural thing to happen. In, out, he made love to her in long, slow strokes. The pace tantalized her and cemented her need for this one perfect man. She rode him in a steady rocking motion, not too fast, but not too slow.

When he released her lips and ducked his head just below the waterline to capture a nipple in his mouth, she nearly came unglued. He played from nipple to nipple, teasing lightly then suckling each in turn deep into his mouth. Caledonia gasped, increasing her pace. She'd wanted him so badly, missed him so much, she couldn't hold out any longer. Struan must've sensed her desperate need.

He lifted from her breast and on a rushed breath stated, "Take a breath, Caledonia." She didn't question. She simply obeyed. Lungs full of air, he released the anchor chain at the same moment he shoved deep into her. Both arms held tight around her waist, holding her snug against him as they sank beneath the surface.

Struan pumped short, hard strokes into her, driving her into the oblivion of the underwater world. If she drowned right now, she'd die a happy woman. Never had she climaxed so intensely as she did with Struan and the water wrapped around her. He throbbed inside her, filling her with his seed. Even though she knew she needed to concentrate on holding her breath she wanted to kiss him. She clasped his face in her hands and laid her lips upon his. They kissed as they floated to the surface, still connected as one.

He broke free of her kiss and pushed the hair back from her eyes. Cupping her chin in his hand, he stared directly at her. "Caledonia, I love you. I know not what path lies before me, but I do know I want you to walk it with me."

Tears threatened to fall and her teeth chattered as the cold water finally seeped through the euphoria of their sexual heat. "I...love...you...too," she stammered.

Struan laughed then placed a kiss to her brow. "Let me get you out o' the loch, my *fiadh-cat,* before you catch a chill."

He guided her to the ladder and shoved her up from behind. His strong hands on her bottom made her shiver even more than the cold of the water. Caledonia scooted over the side and onto the deck. Quickly, she grabbed two oversized bath blankets from one of the storage bins. One she wrapped around herself. The other she handed to Struan the moment he found his footing on deck. He draped it around his shoulders and tugged her into his arms.

"If'n you give me a bit to regain my strength, I want to show you how much more you mean to me."

Caledonia opened her blanket and stepped into his arms. "I plan to hold you to that."

He smiled as he captured her lips. The roar of his stomach made them both burst out laughing, separating their kiss.

"Typical man," Caledonia teased. "Give him sex and all he wants next is food or sleep."

She turned and walked into the wheelhouse. She came out with a picnic basket. "I think you and I were set up. I saw this when we came aboard."

Struan gave her a boyish look that charmed her to her toes. "It seems my *brathairs* may have had enough o' my surly ways without you. Me thinks they may have conspired with your mother in this matter o' the heart."

Caledonia plundered through the basket. Lifting a bottle of wine, two glasses and a corkscrew, she smiled at him. "Me thinks you may be right."

He spread a blanket on the deck, lifted the basket from where Caledonia had set it and placed it between them. They sat facing each other with nothing on but the blankets draped across their shoulders to ward off the cool breeze.

The night slipped past quicker than either would've liked. They ate, drank and talked for hours. It was when Struan asked her to show him how to use the fishing gear that Caledonia knew she'd truly found the perfect man for her. Just like her parents, she and Struan sat out on the loch fishing and enjoying the quite of nature.

A little before sunrise Struan cast out one final time. He was like a kid learning a new toy and not ready to put it away. Caledonia couldn't help but smile at his persistence. She'd caught two tiny trout and released them. Struan hadn't caught anything until now. Something hit the bait the moment it broke the water. Caledonia sprang into action beside him, guiding him on how to best bring the fish in without losing him. Together they tired that fish until they landed him onboard the *Marcail Struana*.

Caledonia's jaw dropped. "Ohmygod, Struan you caught Devil's Disciple!"

"Devil's what?" Struan questioned, holding up the oversized salmon.

"That fish is legend in this loch. Fishermen from miles around—Poppa included—have been after that fish for years. Ohmygod," she gasped excitedly. "Talk about being lucky."

A broad smile split his lips as he worked the hook from the salmon's mouth. "Well then it only stands to reason that a true fisherman should catch him. I say such a prized fish deserves his freedom. For now."

Before she could stop him, Struan released him back into the loch. She stood, mouth gaping wide, staring at him. Struan wiped his hands on the cleaning cloth then took her in his arms.

"Only prize I want from this loch is in my arms right now," he declared in a sultry tone.

Her heart nearly burst with happiness. What a wonderful man she'd fallen in love with. Caledonia wrapped her arms around his neck and captured his mouth in a heated kiss. Together they sank into the mess of blankets on the deck.

Arms and legs tangled together. Struan's fingers knotted in her hair as he clung to her mouth, tasting and savoring the woman he loved. Wine mixed with woman and the natural essence of the loch to fill his taste buds with the flavor that was Caledonia.

He licked and nibbled from her lips to the crevice of her neck then laid a path of hot kisses from breast to breast. Pert nipples teased his tongue and he loved the way she moaned his name softly when he suckled them in deep. It drove her wild and he knew it. She grasped his shaft and guided it home. Her legs locked around his waist, not giving him any option but to follow her frantic pumping action. Never had he known a woman to have such sensitive breasts as his Caledonia.

The harder he tugged and sucked on her breasts, the wilder her hips gyrated beneath him. His little *fiadh-cat* surprised him and managed to buck them over onto his back but he didn't mind. Having her seated on top of him, her hair blanketed around her shoulders, only bound his heart more to hers. She was beautiful. He matched her rocking motion. Slow, then fast, then faster. Her nails dug into his flesh as she gasped for air.

Struan didn't know how much longer he'd last but he knew he was running out of time. The sun threatened to penetrate the early-morning sky. Pain gripped his heart like a fist held it and squeezed. Sweat beaded his brow and upper lip. His skin sizzled but he couldn't stop. He needed one second more with Caledonia before he'd succumb to the curse. He closed his eyes against the pain, causing stars to dance behind his lids. His guess about how the curse was broken must've been wrong.

"Caledonia, I love you," he professed wanting to make sure she knew the truth of his heart before the curse took him. *Or he died*, flashed behind his eyes for a split second due to the severity of the pain slicing through his chest. If death lay on his horizon, then let him die happily in the arms of the woman he loved, he conceded.

Her breasts bounced enticingly. He couldn't resist. Wrapping an arm around her waist, he sat upright, seating himself fully within her channel as he clasped onto one of her magnificent breasts. Caledonia screamed his name, sending it echoing across the loch. Wave upon wave, her sheath contracted, beckoning him to join her phenomenal release. His cock twitched as his bawls constricted, releasing his seed deep within his *fiadh-cat*. Never had he come so strongly or been so completely drained.

He lay back, cradling her against his chest. Just one more second and he'd have no choice but to push her off before the sun… Struan opened his eyes at the odd sensation upon his face. Heat from the first glimmer of the sun's rays danced over the rail of the boat and caressed his skin. Holding his hand before his eyes, reality hit.

The curse was broken.

"Caldonia," he whispered excitedly against the top of her head.

"Umm," she mumbled in a totally satisfied tone.

"Open your eyes, my love."

He knew the moment she realized the same thing he did. She sat upright, mouth dropped open and eyes wide. "You didn't change. Ohmygod, Struan. The curse."

"We broke it." He sat up, taking her into his arms.

She leaned back, staring straight into his eyes. The hottest, sexiest colored eyes he'd ever seen almost glowed with excitement as she proclaimed on a rushed breath. "Love breaks the curse. That's what your family was trying to tell us without telling us."

"Aye," he said as he nodded. "Seems we had to accept it for ourselves for the curse to break."

The weight of Caledonia throwing herself against him toppled them backward as they laughed.

"I love you, my *fiadh-cat*. My beautiful Caledonia."

"And I love you, Struan. Now and forever."

* * * * *

From the shore, two men stood at the end of a dock. One searched the loch for a boat named *Marcail Struana*. Upon finding it, he adjusted the borrowed pirate spyglass and saw exactly what he hoped. He lowered the glass, turned to his *brathair* and grinned.

"It worked?" Ian questioned Gavin.

"Aye." He nodded as he answered. "Seems another MacKinnon *brathair* is free."

ABOUT THE AUTHOR

Tara Nina creates in a variety of ranges from steamy hot to simmering sweet, which includes paranormals, contemporaries, suspense and sci-fi. She's a Southerner living in the northern wilds of New Jersey complete with grown children, two dogs, six turtles and a mountain man for a husband.

She loves to hear from readers so feel free to contact her via email tara@taranina.com

Please don't get discouraged if it takes a little while before she responds. Unfortunately, she hasn't hit the lottery yet and has to work to battle the bills of home ownership. Being a full-time writer is on her bucket list and one day, she hopes to achieve that goal.

Join her Clan MacKinnon Fan Club/Newsletter for updates on what's new and exciting in her world. http://taranina.com/join-the-clan/

Check out her website http://taranina.com

She is also available on the following media outlets:

Facebook: https://www.facebook.com/TaraNinaAuthor

Twitter: https://twitter.com/taranina

Pinterest: https://www.pinterest.com/taranina/

Instagram: https://www.instagram.com/taranina1

<u>OTHER TITLES BY TARA NINA</u>

CURSE OF THE GARGOYLE
(CURSED MACKINNONS BOOK 1)

EYES OF STONE
(CURSED MACKINNONS BOOK 2)

MOUNTAIN MEN
(BROTHERS DUPREE)

MINDWARP

ALL I WANT FOR CHRISTMAS IS A MARINE